See what happens to Eddie Slate the day the oil runs out...

"Strap in and buckle up. Gripping and apocalyptic
~Readerman's Bookshelf

"A catastrophic event, a woman gone missing, and a ruthless killer who will stop at nothing to get what he wants... Chilling."
~The Word Factory

"Twists and turns like a rollercoaster... Unstoppable."
~Salington Press

"Bolt the doors and board up the windows... J.L. Davis digs deep into the psychological mind of a killer and the everyday man's struggle for survival in a world gone wild."
~Daily Bookworm

"Pulse-pounding. Two BIG thumbs up!"
~ Mark Rainstone Reviews

CRUDE

RAINFIRE PUBLISHING

All Rights Reserved

Cover Art and Design: Marybeth Cauley

Illustrative Consultant: Jake Rocco

Cynthia.

Welcome to the New World Order . —

[handwritten signature]

CRUDE
a novel by J.L. Davis

Thanks to Marybeth Cauley for her inspiration, dreams of thunder and life on a beach under the shooting stars.

Also Eddie Tout, a.k.a. master computer technician, for all the adventures and years of friendship.

... and for Trooper Pompa, long time friend down at Soundcheck Records, one of the last great independent record stores in America.

Also for Doug Rontz in memory of all those excursions to The Molly's.

... and of course to all my family and friends, with special thanks to Nadine Suchon Schmidt and Anne Davis Shupp for all their support.

Last but never least, for everyone gassing up the cars, turning up the radio and jetting off to Acapulco. Hold on tight to your dreams... they go on forever.

Contents

Live from the Dakota
The Author's Commentary

Live from the Dakota
From the Author's Cellar

I first thought about writing CRUDE while standing on 78th street in New York, next to the Dakota building. The day was cold. People hurried up and down the avenue, their coats bundled around them in the blustery weather. A man with a scruffy beard and long overcoat stood beside me on a corner eating a hot dog.

"Hey man." Swallowing hard, he pointed at the Dakota. "You know what happened here, don't you?"

I shrugged. I was in the Big Apple exploring the dinosaurs in the Natural History Museum. Later in the afternoon, I took a walk around Central Park. Somewhere in my travels I ended up in front of the Dakota.

"You remember The Beatles?" he said. "John Lennon took a bullet, right here in front of this building. It makes you wonder what kind of a world we live in when a guy like that can get gunned down on a busy street corner."

I was young but remembered that night. Mark David Chapman fired five shots in front of the Dakota, four of which landed in Lennon's back. The suspect remained on the scene reading a J.D. Salinger novel until the police arrived and arrested him.

"People are crazy," the stranger with the beard said. "Imagine the anarchy if something really big happened. What if all the power grids in the city failed and never came back on? People turn into wolves in the dark. It would be Katrina all over again."

The guy was a strange bird but he had a point. Katrina was one of the strongest hurricanes to ever make landfall in the United States. The storm surged over twenty feet and eighty percent of New Orleans flooded after the levees breached. From the streets to the Superdome, stories of brutality filled the evening news. Plain and simple, people went crazy.

A few nights later on a chilly November evening, I stared out the window of my house. The last of the fall leaves, blazing with red and yellow colors, drooped and littered the ground. Frost hung in the air and settled on the grass and automobile windshields. Soon winter would be upon us.

Sitting down on the couch, I picked up the remote and flicked through the television channels. I must have dozed off because the next thing I remembered was waking up in the middle of the night with heavy winds rattling the house. Peering out the window, the American flag that hung from a mast at the Diligent Fire Company flapped in the blustery weather.

Just up the road, my eyes widened when a big oak toppled over. In a tremendous crash it hit electrical wires on a telephone pole. Sparks flew and fire whistles sounded. Seconds later, the lights flickered and the power went out.

It didn't take long for the house to get cold. After lighting a candle, I slipped on my coat and stepped outside. An emergency vehicle with a rotating beacon lumbered up the road.

Hitting the brakes, a utility worker with a hard hat got out of a truck to survey the damage.

"How bad is it?" I yelled.

"Bad enough," He shined a flashlight on a broken wire extending down the side of the telephone pole.

"When will we get power back?"

"Not sure," he said. "The wind is killing us. We got outages all over the county."

I went back into the house, poured myself a drink and sat down on the recliner. Staring at the candle flickering against the wall, I found myself thinking about the stranger at the Dakota in New York.

"Imagine the anarchy if all the power grids failed. It'd be Katrina all over again." His voice echoed in my head.

That statement made me stop and think about things. What if disaster, a wild tiger in the jungle, caught us off guard and struck before we ever had a chance to mount a defense? How would people survive if suddenly everything they've ever known was gone?

I didn't have a lot of time to think about it. At that moment the lights went on, the refrigerator began to hum and the old furnace sputtered and started running . It was just that quick; life became normal again.

Looking back, that's the time I began to think about writing CRUDE. I began to wonder what might happen if something unforeseen, a natural catastrophe or some other unworldly means, unexpectedly struck and turned the human race on its head.

Don't worry. For today, this minute, this hour, you're secure without threat of harm or consequence. You can hum your favorite tune on the radio, grab a beer after work at the local pub or turn up the thermostat on a cold wintry night. For today do whatever makes you happy, because sure as hell, tomorrow is coming fast.

Now sit down and get comfortable. If just for a little while, we're going to leave today behind. We're going to shut down the furnace, turn off the lights and pull the plug on the refrigerator. Suddenly everything you've ever known in life will be gone.

The time is now and the place, your hometown. See you in thirty days.

~ It's the things we don't see coming that we choose to ignore.

1

Out go the Lights

"Hello?"

Empty static.

"Is anyone there, anyone at all?"

Dead silence.

I can't be certain but I swear someone muttered something on the radio. Okay, so sometimes I hear things. Boards squeak and rats shuffle in the wall. I get scared. Nobody can fault me for that. I was a car salesman, not a cop in downtown Detroit. Saturday nights were spent watching a ball game and drinking a cold one over at The Molly's. That was thirty days ago. Things changed since then.

These days I spend my time hunkered down in the cellar of my house. The hours are empty. I stare at walls. Pick my teeth. Lately my major source of entertainment is a spider clinging to a cobweb draped over a bent nail on the ceiling. I know. It isn't dinner at Carmine's in New York, but it's safer and less terrifying than the constant ring of sporadic gunfire in the street.

A garbled voice again came over the radio.

"Hello?" I clutched the receiver. "I know you're out there. Talk to me!"

Nobody answered. Not one damned person.

Still I know someone's listening. You know the feeling, right? You're in a checkout line at the grocery store and it hits you. Bam! You're being scoped. That's what I'm talking about; even though I can't see the ghost in the darkness, I know it's out there.

Crouched at the bottom of the cellar steps, a rifle cradled in my arms, I peered up the staircase that led to the first floor of the house. Maybe somebody got inside. I boarded up all the entrances and windows, but people, especially the bad ones, are persistent.

"Can you hear me?" I shouted up the steps. "I got a gun. Don't test me!"

Listening close, the only sound was broken shudders flapping in the cold wind.

Sighing, I loosened my grip on the gun.

When it comes right down to it, I avoid going outside ever since the lights went out. These days my house has become a refuge, not just from the cold, but the monsters that people sometimes become. Peeking out from behind cracks in the boarded up windows, at times I wonder if help will ever arrive.

Regardless, I haven't given up on my dreams. That's what I hang on to these days: dreams.

Man, back when I was a kid? I thought I'd be a movie star. Yup, that's me. I'd cruise around Tinsel Town in an expensive Armani suit and Rayban sunglasses. Maybe book a room at the Sunset Towers and sip margaritas with some beautiful woman at my side as the waves crashed against the beach. Yeah, I was really gonna be a big shot. The thing of it is, right about now? I'd give it all up for a bar of soap, a shower and a hot meal.

My name is Eddie Slate. It began on a Monday, about 30 days ago. I hated Mondays, a new work week and all that crap. There weren't many customers around that day. For the most part I stood in the lobby drinking Starbucks and paging through a bent up paperback novel called *Nesting with the Loons* that I found stuffed in the magazine rack. Business was slow. It was about to get a lot slower.

"What the hell?" My boss, Fred Hanna, blurted out from inside his office.

"You talking to me?" I craned my neck around.

"Turn on CNN."

"What?"

"Turn it on!" He repeated loudly. "We got trouble."

Grabbing the TV remote, I flicked through the channels. It didn't take long to find the news.

A commentator with a five o'clock shadow cleared his throat. "We're getting confirmation at the federal levels Carl," he said to his co-anchor. Dabbing at his forehead with a monogrammed handkerchief, he stared at the teleprompter. "Saudi Arabia, Russia, Iran. Major refineries all over the world are reporting massive deficits in CRUDE production."

"That's right Bill," his co-anchor jumped in. "Oil rigs from the Gulf of Mexico to South Africa are sucking drops." He loosened his red tie which on any other morning would have looked dapper against his Brooks Brother's suit. "Crude production is down seventy percent and dropping faster than the stock market after 911." Pausing, he stared at the camera. "There is no oil left."

News of the disaster played out gentle as a terrorist dropping a bomb on Manhattan. According to reports, the government had secretly been aware of the problem for over two years. Bent on averting public panic, authorities kept the situation secret, hoping that companies like OPEC might find a solution to the disaster. They didn't.

"This just in," the commentator said. "Tankers carrying payloads of crude are being recalled back home by foreign governments." The cameras cut to huge freighters on the move across the Atlantic. It wouldn't be long until other large ships, moving from port to port in search of petroleum, ran out of fuel and drifted with the currents like lost and floating islands. Again the commentator dabbed at beads of sweat on his forehead. "If things don't change quickly, this could be just the beginning of the storm."

That, of course, was an understatement.

Before the day ended, 50,000 planes that took off anywhere between Los Angeles and Beijing would be cancelled. Trillions of dollars in oil stock would be instantly worthless and the board of directors at places like Chevron and BP would be tearing out what little hair was left on their heads. Wealthy investors on Wall Street, the big shots with beach houses down in Malibu, were probably already leaning out the window of the 5th floor at the Bank of New York ready to take the plunge.

Scrunching up my empty cup from Starbucks, I tossed it in the trash and looked out the window.

Across the road, cars piled up at a self-service gas station. The line extended out of the parking lot and down the street, nearly to Antonio's pizza shop. Long before the day ended, the pumps would be spitting air.

"Slate, are you listening?" The boss shouted and ran out of his office. Cords of stress, wire thick, stretched across his forehead.

"I don't get it." I stared out the window at the self service station, now flooded with determined and frightened customers. "Oil can't just stop. This has to be a joke."

"Are you an idiot?" the boss said. Even in a crisis, the bastard loved to insult me. "Look at the TV." Grabbing the remote, he clicked through five or six stations, all of which reported on the oil crunch, and then tossed the changer on a chair. "Satisfied? Everything from cooking shows to Kathy Lee and Hoda has been cancelled. The government is refusing to comment on whether or not they'll ration out the reserves. Leave it to the feds to be evasive, right?"

It was true. Instead of economic reports, national deficits and worldwide terrorism, a new kid on the block took center stage.

"Lock the place up." The boss tossed me the keys. "Sure as hell we won't be selling any cars today."

No argument there. When you think about it, the automobile industry probably isn't the business of choice in an oil crisis. Then again, what was?

"More fallout Bill." The newscaster sucked nervously at his lips. "Manufacturers across the nation are shutting down. We have reports of riots at the gas pumps from Newark to Sacramento. We've never seen anything like this." The commentator opened his mouth again but quickly closed it.

How much was there left to say? Businesses driven by fuel came to a crashing halt and confused workers punched out for a permanent vacation. Talk about a goddamn unemployment rate. Millions would be jobless before the noon whistle.

With the economy in the throes of collapse, banks shelling out money to edgy clientele who worried about their life savings would soon go broke. The freaking F.D.I.C. would be hung from a tall tree when the public figured out that having their money insured had about the same impact as a jumbo jet flying in the middle of the Indian Ocean with no fuel. Odds of making it back to dry land were at best, bleak.

"Something tells me the chaos hasn't even begun," the commentator concluded.

All of this and it was still the first morning of the end of the civilized world.

2

Comforts of a Cellar Lifestyle

On the morning that things went bad, I hurried out of work, drove down the road and slammed on the brakes at a red light, just outside of Elmo's Market. Craning my head around, I could see in the front window of the store. Food lines at the registers stretched the length of the aisles. People's faces were ghosted over with dread.

I'm not sure how seriously I took it. A snow squall filtering in from the Great Lakes had everyone emptying the bread and milk shelves as if it were the end of the world. But this wasn't a whiteout during a winter storm. This was more like an asteroid strike in the Yucatan Peninsula. It had the potential for permanent disaster, and at the moment, we all might as well have all been dinosaurs.

Food and water would get scarce. Stockpiled with produce, thousands of trucks left places like Florida and California en route to countrywide deliveries. With no place to fuel up the rigs, the industry would be in dire straits.

I glanced over at Elmo's. An elderly man, mid seventies, stood on the sidewalk clutching a box of cereal.

"You stole that." An Italian woman glared and pointed an angry finger.

Speechless and frightened, the old man said nothing.

"Give it back." The Italian woman pulled the goods from the old man's hands and walked briskly down the street.

The traffic light at Elmo's turned green and I hit the gas. Just up the road, over by Pine Avenue, a retired school bus driver named Henry Gates stood by a hedge in his yard. Henry wasn't your everyday NRA representative. He was a staunch democrat who opposed the use of firearms. Still there he stood, a pistol stuffed in his trousers, eyeing me with a weary face. In as little as hours since the broadcast declaring the oil disaster, the most basic social principles had fallen into decay.

Not wasting any time, I sped down the street and turned left on Center Avenue. Swinging my car into the driveway, I hurried up the front lawn and bolted myself in the house.

I own a gun, did I mention that? I hate the damn things, but a few years back a shady salesman convinced me to purchase one for home defense.

"Nice action on this puppy." A shyster with a goatee blew on the barrel.

I scratched my head. "I don't know. It might not be a good idea. I don't like guns."

"Don't be stupid." He shoved the weapon in my hands. "Someday this'll save your life."

The rifle is a .223 Remington. I don't know what that means but then it probably doesn't matter. I never had the guts to fire it, but something tells me I better change that mindset. Dangerous people are everywhere, and if we ever get out of this mess, the NRA should run an add justifying the use of arms in America.

Regardless, I keep my rifle cribbed in my arms, a scare tactic to ward off looters and other forms of uninvited guests.

Don't get me wrong. I don't like confrontation and would avoid the use of firearms even if I had a full chamber and an open target. If someone broke into the house, I'd cower in the cellar until they went away, that is, if they went away. In the meantime, if the government ever decides to stand up and be counted, help should arrive in the form of FEMA or the National Guard, riding in on white stallions and restoring law and order. The thing is, with no fuel for transportation, first they'd need to build the wagons and train the horse teams.

I'm telling you, sometimes I have to laugh. I really have to laugh. I used to listen to all the experts on the History Channel talk about alien invasions and rogue asteroids. Too bad all the ancient astronaut theorists weren't as concerned about oil fields in the Gulf as some little green Martian making crop circles in Glasgow England.

Not me though. I kept the refrigerator stockpiled and bottled water in the basement. A few weeks ago I even bought a couple of cases of MRE's from the army store down in Dover. They taste like cardboard but last long. I guess listening to all those doomsday criers spouting off about the end times finally paid off. Starvation, at least for the moment, isn't on the menu.

My thoughts were interrupted by a noise on the radio.

"Hello?"

No answer.

"Can you hear me?"

Muddied in static, someone laughed.

"You think this is funny?" I gripped the radio. "Stop playing games. Who is this?"

Holding the receiver close to my ear, I listened close. Barely audible but unmistakable, there was a sound more frightening than any words ever spoken.

On the other end of the radio, I could hear someone breathing.

3

The girl I used to Know

Even before the electric shutdown, most of the physical and social infrastructure broke. People were stranded on subways and long distance commuters, out of gas, abandoned their cars against guardrails on the turnpike. Most television stations went off the air but major news networks like CNN managed to continue broadcasting, at least periodically.

Shuffling some disheveled papers on a desk, a commentator stared wearily into the camera. "More weather woes. What do you got Megan?"

The meteorologist cleared her throat. She was a beautiful young woman but not even makeup could hide the dark circles underneath her eyes. She pushed back a strand of hair that hung irritably down the middle of her forehead. "There's a classic nor'easter rolling in from Canada. A lot of ice associated with this one. Power lines could go down. If that happens..."

Suddenly the channel turned to snow.

"Come on!" I banged a fist on the television.

Grabbing the remote, I flicked through the stations. All the networks were off the air. Either the boys down at the cable company took an early lunch or they decided to punch out and go home until the world came back online. I picked up the phone but that didn't work either. It was official; communication had been reduced to radio and short range transmissions.

I can tell you what the real kicker is about all of this. Those bastards forecasting the weather couldn't predict sun in a bright blue sky let alone a major ice storm in late November. Global warming would keep the temperatures on the upswing, right?

Wrong.

Two days later the sky turned dark as ashes. It got cold. Damn cold. Soon the ice came. I stood in the kitchen listening to it pelt the rainspout and roof. Minutes later the lights flickered and went out. Take it from someone who knows. You don't realize how much you miss the hum of a refrigerator until it stops. Lighting a candle, I set it on the kitchen table.

Since then, there hasn't been much to do in the empty hours but stare at walls. That, and of course dream about what life was like before things fell apart. Looking back, I'd bet everyone in the world knew exactly where they were on that day. It's kind of like falling in love for the first time; nobody forgets stuff like that.

The first time I took the plunge was with a girl named Beth Andrews. She had long dark hair and blue eyes, shiny as diamonds in the sun. Our first date was at a high school dance. A band named Macbeth Periscope played. Man, those guys really knew how to ramp it up. After the dance, we drove to Chunk Lake. I grabbed a blanket out of the car and we cuddled up on the beach under the stars.

"I got a surprise," she told me one night before she got out of my car. "I got you a present."

"A present?"

She pulled it out of a bag. "It's a radio."

"A radio?" I scratched my head stupidly.

She smiled, her eyes glittering in moonlight. "My father had them stocked away in a box down in the cellar. I thought it might be fun to try them. You can never tell when all the power will go out and you'll want to call me." Kissing me on the cheek, she jumped out of the car, turned and smiled, then hurried in the house.

I swear to God I loved that girl, even if she was crazy.

And I did call Beth on the radio more than once in the middle of the night when I couldn't sleep. The sound of her voice, soft and melodic, had this kind of healing effect on my soul that always made me fall back into a dream.

That was my summer of love. A few months later, Beth went off to college in Pittsburgh and we drifted apart. It happens, you know? People disappear out of each other's lives. In the end she married an accountant and relocated to the West Coast. But the marriage didn't last and some years later she returned home. We didn't live far apart, but I guess those sweet romantic teenage nights passed us by. We never rekindled that youthful love affair.

But you know something? I always kept that stupid radio she gave me when we were kids. Sitting here in the dark and staring at it, sometimes I wonder if rather than an endearing teenage gift, it was meant as a foreshadowing of the dark days to come.

"Beth Andrews?" I talked to myself on the radio. I guess I'm just a glutton for punishment. "It's Eddie Slate, remember me? We used to park at the beach when we were teenagers. The good old days, right? I still got this old radio you gave me all those years ago and thought I'd give you a call. How about coming over to my place for a romantic dinner by candlelight? We can celebrate the end of the world."

I stared dumbly at the transmitter, listened to empty static, and laughed.

What the hell was I doing? Going crazy, that's what.

Trust me. You don't know what it's like living in a cellar with no electric, no heat, nobody to talk to. You might think you know, but you don't.

Some years ago my mother unexpectedly passed away from cancer. On the nights that followed, I'd watch my father sitting in his recliner in the living-room. He'd stare emptily at the television, his face ghosted over with all the things he loved and lost. One night I saw him sitting in the dark all alone in that room, staring at nothing. After awhile, folding his head in his hands, he silently wept.

That's what I'm talking about. Looking at my reflection in the musty mirror upstairs, that's what I see staring back at me. I swear that sometimes it feels as if I'm dissolving inside, lost as a stone thrown out to sea and drifting with the currents. I spend the hours walking from room to room, humming old songs and talking to myself. I try to be strong, tough as nails, but every now and then? Not unlike my father seated in a darkened room reminiscing about the life he once knew, I fall apart.

"You hear that Beth?" I again said in the radio. "I could use a little company tonight. I guess we both could."

For a moment I heard something, a garbled voice, deep and throaty.

"Who is this?" I raised a suspicious brow.

The radio got quiet again.

I could be hearing things again. It happens. When you spend too much time alone, you lose perspective on reality. Still there is something I'm certain about. At times I get that eerie sensation of being spied on. It's as if someone in the shadows, someone unseen, has a finger on my pulse.

Another garbled sound came over the radio.

"I know you're out there." I gripped the radio. "Identify yourself! What do you want from me?"

And then it came, quiet as a soft footed kitten.

"I'm coming for you," someone whispered.

4

Out on the Streets

Staring at the radio, my face drew a blank. Someone had been eavesdropping. Toying with me. Listening to my every word.

I looked around, suspicious that a thief might have found a way into the house.

"Is someone up there?" I shouted up the cellar steps. "I have a gun!"

Silence hung in the air, stagnant and thick as pools of black smoke.

Taking a deep breath, I tried to calm down. It was probably nothing but the wind. Yeah, that had to be it. Either that or I my mind was playing tricks again.

The truth is that I couldn't take much more of talking to walls and began to consider starvation or a well placed bullet to the head as an attractive alternative to the cellar lifestyle. Regardless of the danger, I decided to venture outside the house and see firsthand what the world had become.

The crawlspace in my cellar led to a shoot underneath the wooden deck in my backyard. Man, now that's a memory. I used to throw some great 4th of July barbecues out there. Closing my eyes, I can still hear steaks sizzling on the grill.

Whenever I screw up the courage to leave the house, I shimmy through the crawlspace and exit out the coal shoot to avoid detection from unwanted eyes.

It was just after midnight that I found myself standing in the backyard of the house. Ice glistened on the front lawn. Looking wearily from side to side, I pulled out the radio and held it to my ear. A steady buzz hummed over the receiver. Whoever had been transmitting must have signed off.

"You hear that Beth?" I said in the radio. "It looks like we're all alone." I looked up at the sky dotted with stars. A host of fleeting clouds dabbed the moon. "It's a romantic night, even if it is the end of civilization. I got some kerosene in the cellar that I stole from Marvin Sterling's shanty. What do you say we cuddle up and reminisce about the old days when we still had cell phones and hot showers?"

I stared blankly at the transmitter and started to laugh.

What was I doing? Nobody was on radio, least of all Beth. My psychological makeup stood in doubt and mental status, unclear. I was slowly going crazy.

"You got that right," said the little subconscious guy in my mind. *"You're losing your mind."*

"No I'm not," I argued.

"Trust me, you are."

"I'm not!"

"You are!"

Who the hell cares.

Pulling my coat tight around me as a shield against icy winds, I noticed a baseball bat tossed on the ground by a rusted out swimming pool in Malone's yard. Picking it up, a smile the size of the East Coast cracked my lips. I don't want to brag, but I used to pound softballs down at Sam Miller's field. I could swing like a son of a bitch. Sometimes I'd hit the ball so hard she'd fly over the rear fence into Barrett's yard. Those were carefree days filled with youth and magic, but now? Sam Miller's field is empty and vacant as a dead man's eyes, and peering into the darkened streets, I knew how a soldier must feel as he assesses his chance for survival on a battlefield. The world looked foreign and alien, and the only use for a wooden bat leftover from the great American pastime was clear: resistance and defense.

Gripping the bat tight in my hands, I kept moving.

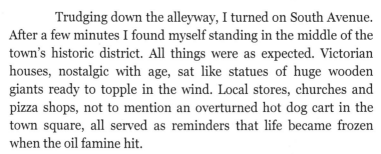

Trudging down the alleyway, I turned on South Avenue. After a few minutes I found myself standing in the middle of the town's historic district. All things were as expected. Victorian houses, nostalgic with age, sat like statues of huge wooden giants ready to topple in the wind. Local stores, churches and pizza shops, not to mention an overturned hot dog cart in the town square, all served as reminders that life became frozen when the oil famine hit.

"Beth?" I said in the radio again. "I'm downtown, near The Rainbow House. Remember when we'd come here on Saturday afternoons and walk around all the junk shops? Man, things changed. We won't be sitting in the Gazebo in the park any longer. Someone burned the damn thing to the ground."

I stopped in mid stride at the sound of heavy boots approaching. Someone stood in the alley between two tenements. Quickly I took cover behind a pickup truck parked in front of the National Bank.

A stranger came out of a side-street. He had a rifle flung over his shoulder and a bottle of whiskey dangling in his hand. Pulling out a cigarette from a beat up leather jacket, he flicked a lighter, lit up, and then walked in the front door of Soundcheck Records, a local downtown music store.

I heard someone arguing followed by the clap of a gunshot and a flash of light discharging from a rifle. A minute later, the stranger stepped back out of the door. Looking up and down the street, he sniffed at the night air and then sauntered away.

Peering across the road, everything grew quiet. I crept alongside the truck and then hurried across the street. Peering into the window of the music store, I didn't see any movement. A friend of mine, Leo Giannetti, owned the place. There's a memory; sometimes we'd stand around the store for hours yakking it up about the old days.

"Soundcheck Records is one the last independent record stores in America, but things aren't up to par these days." Leo sifted through some boxes of old records brought in by the locals for five bucks a bundle. "I've been in this business thirty years," he complained. "Thirty goddamn years and I never saw things so screwed up." Pulling a vintage Beatles album out from behind the counter, he polished the record sleeve with a bottle of window cleaner. "You wanna know whose fault it is? I'll tell you whose fault it is. It's the corporate giants." He answered his own question. "They're the evil empire, but you know something?" He got huffy. "I won't let those bastards drive me out of business. I got passion. You know what that is?" He wrapped his knuckles on his chest. "I love this freaking music store, and I'm telling you, the only way they'll get me to close down is to carry me out in a box."

That statement turned out to be prophetic.

An OPEN sign hung in the front window of the store and the door stood ajar. I cautiously stepped inside to have a look around. DVD's were scattered on the floor, and a magazine rack, spilled over.

"Anybody home?" I said.

Turning my head towards the cash register, I gasped. A dark figure sat behind the counter.

"Leo?" I scrunched the bat tight in my fists. "Hey man, is that you?"

Taking a step closer, I gasped.

Slumped on a stool with a vintage Eddie and the Cruisers album lodged in his hands, Leo stared into the darkness. A bullet hole squared up in his head, his dormant eyes looked as unmoving as grave markers.

The sight was so disarming that it staggered me backwards, but my hardened expression quickly melted into liquid fear. Someone fired a gunshot in the streets. The bullet shattered the store's front window; it landed in a wall, just above a Billboard poster advertising this month's hot 100 hits. A second round splintered the front door and ricochet past my ear.

I hit the floor, belly down. Sweat pooled on my forehead. Looking out the door,, a gunman lingered in the shadows, just across the street. The tip of his cigarette glowed in the sunken darkness and the sharp clap of a rifle being reloaded reverberated in the night air.

My stomach twisted in knots. I was being scoped.

5

The Man with the Silver Bullet

Unless you've been stalked, you don't know how it feels. You're carrying groceries to the car or coming out of the restroom at a local restaurant. It hits you. Someone's watching. Be it an anonyms follower or casual acquaintance, you're targeted. Obsession takes over. The person sits outside in the shadows for hours, preoccupied with your every move. It happens. I even had a neighbor who became so obsessed with his ex-wife that he collected her hair from the shower drain. Mostly they're harmless individuals who eventually move on. Peering out the window of the record shop with a bullet hole in the window, something told me this one wouldn't.

I looked around the room and searched for an exit. The store had a backdoor. I could make a run for it. The thing is, if he saw me, the game would be over. Sure as hell the guy wasn't looking for white wine and sparkling conversation. I'd have a shell in my head before I ever turned the doorknob.

Craning my head to see, I peered out the door again. Litter tumbled down the sidewalk in the wind but nothing else moved. Still impending doom knotted up my gut. At any second, a gunman might crash through the entrance, his boots crunching glass from the shattered storefront window.

Crouching behind a stack of empty boxes, I waited for the hammer to crack the wood. But instead of a gunman toting a loaded rifle intent on spraying bullets, the only sound I heard was crackling on the radio.

"Hey Eddie, pick up if you're there," someone said.

I pulled the radio out of my pocket and stared blankly at it. "Hello?"

"Eddie Slate? Cool beans. I thought you signed off."

I tilted my head distrustfully. "Do I know you?"

"You were on the radio earlier. I heard you say your name. Man, I haven't heard a friendly voice in weeks."

"Where are you?" I asked. "Anywhere near the historic district?"

"Sure am."

"Listen to me. I need help."

"What's wrong?"

"You know the music store downtown?"

"Yes, but..."

"Just listen." I cut him off. "I'm trapped in the store. Some maniac is running around outside."

"There's a lot of that going on these days."

"This one got a rifle." I glanced at Leo, slouched behind the cash register. "I think he killed the store owner."

"Really?"

"He got a bullet hole in his head."

"Well," he paused. "I wouldn't worry too much."

I blinked uncertainly. "What are you talking about?"

"Headshots are quick and painless."

"Are you crazy?" I asked. "He murdered the guy."

"Don't be so damn sensitive." The person's tone, much like a chameleon, suddenly changed. "With the funk the music business is in these days, I did him a favor."

My heart froze. "You killed him?"

"Please, hold the applause." He laughed. "The goddamn world is a disaster zone and that crazy bastard was polishing records when I walked in. He caught me off guard sitting alone in the dark like that. Hell, I guess nobody comes out in the daylight these days. What we got is a nation of vampires, and me? I'm just the man with the silver bullet."

A cold chill dampened the back of my neck. "I'm warning you. Don't come near me." I tightened my grip on the wooden bat.

"Take it easy," the stranger said. "If I wanted you dead, the cutting crew would already be trimming the grass around your headstone."

"What do you want from me?"

"On the radio you said you had food Eddie. You said you had lots of food."

I shook my head. Yup, I had to admit it. Luck wasn't my best attribute. If I ever hit it rich, I'd either lose the lottery ticket or a greedy banker would embezzle the money. Still, after sleeping on cold cement floors and scrounging in garbage cans for food, I remained optimistic. I waited for the National Guard, FEMA, or perhaps even a backyard survivalist to come and ease my plight, but instead got a poacher with a loaded gun and a bad attitude.

"Sorry man," I said. "My supplies are just about gone."

"Don't lie to me Eddie. Can I call you Eddie?"

I couldn't figure it out. By the way he talked you'd swear we were old high school buddies.

"I'm telling the truth. I'm empty."

"You must think I'm pretty damn stupid, don't you?" Resentment swirled in his voice. "What's the problem? I just need a little food and water. Is that so bad? It's not like I'm trying to screw your girlfriend, what's her name again, Beth?"

I stared dumbly at the transmitter. He must have listened to every word I said over the radio.

"Tell me something Eddie," he forged ahead. "Is Beth your lover or maybe just some cheap two dollar whore from over on 5th street?"

"Shut your mouth," I said angrily. "You don't know anything about her."

"That's where you're wrong cowboy. I know she's a nice rack of lamb." He whistled. "You know what I'd do with a woman like that? I'd give her a night at the opera Eddie. You know, make her moan, maybe sing Felicia. By morning she'd have a satisfied smile six miles to sunset, and then afterwards?" He paused to consider. "I'd kill her Eddie. I'd kill her slow. I'd make it hurt."

A cold chill ran down my spine. The guy on the radio wasn't just mean or brutal. He was certifiable.

"The conversation is over," I told him. "I'm getting off the radio."

"Now you're being rude. You're pushing me cowboy," he warned. "I'll bet you wouldn't talk to Beth that way."

"You're crazy," I said. "You want to kill me? I got no food, water, heat and electric, or even a working toilet. And you think shooting me is a punishment?" I almost laughed. "If you want to put a bullet in me, come on over."

"Because Eddie, I'm not downtown anymore," the gunman said. "I'm just down the road, standing in front of Beth's house. You see, I have her tied up in the bedroom, and unless you bring me food and supplies in the next few minutes?" He paused. "She's dead."

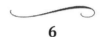

6

Heroes

I stared at the radio, listening to empty static. He had to be lying. Then again, I announced Beth's name on the radio. He could have heard me and picked up a phonebook. Found her address and paid her a visit.

"Are you still there?" Vapors of cold frost hung in the air from my breath. "Hello?"

The line remained dead.

I bit at my fingernails, contemplating the next move. It was dark outside. I could go to Beth's house. Stay undercover. Hide in the hedges and watch the parameter for movement.

"What the hell are you thinking?" My subconscious barked. "You'd *be walking into to trap. Food is harder to come by these days than moon rocks. This guy would beat you into submission inside of a minute. Go home and call it a day."*

Icy wind whipped through the open door of the record shop, stinging my cheeks. Pulling out my flashlight, I shined it around the room. The light reflected in Leo's marble eyes. Beside him, a vintage record player sat on a counter with a beat up Meatloaf album beside it. Dressed in high-tops and big hair, as a kid I nearly blew the speakers out of my dad's car listening to that thing out at the lake.

Looking back, that's where I first kissed Beth on a warm summer night. Her lips, moist and perfect, tasted like fresh strawberries. Man, that night was magic; you know what I'm talking about? I had a tingly sensation from my toes to my ears all the while this stupid little voice in the back of my head kept saying, *"Don't blow it Eddie. She's the one."*

One night on the beach we saw a shooting star and made a wish that we'd always be together. I pulled her close and said, "I'd do anything in the world for you Beth."

"I know you would Eddie." She softly kissed my cheek. "You'd always come to my rescue."

Wrapping my arm around her, we held each other deep into the night.

My daydream shattered at the sound of a distant gunshot. Getting up, I hurried out the door of the music store. I couldn't shake the thought, or the guilt, of saying Beth's name over the radio. How damn stupid was I to do that? It put her life in peril.

A few years ago I went to my class reunion. A girl named Valerie Becker was there. Sporting dark hair and a golden tan, she walked in the place wearing a purple sequined lace dress that melted every guy to the floor like candle wax. I bumped into her after the gathering.

"Hey Valerie," I said. "Everyone's headed up to the lake. We figured we'd relive the submarine races. It'll be a last blast leftover from our youth." I laughed. "Wanna come?"

Valerie smiled. "It's late." She hung tight to her fiancé, Peter Sloan, a law student at Penn.

Outside of the reunion hall, a couple of guys dressed in burgundy suits and cheap sunglasses whooped it up.

"The animals are restless tonight." Valerie giggled and paused. "Okay," she conceded. "We'll stop for a few minutes."

Valerie Becker was a free spirit. She loved the ballet and sometimes performed at small venues across the state. The girl had this dream about being a dancer and lighting up the stage on Broadway. But fate, a hurricane about to make landfall, had other plans.

On the way to the lake, a truck lost its brakes on the Wash Shanty Hill. It rammed Peter Sloan's sleek red convertible, headfirst. Picture a tin can collapsing under the weight of a sledgehammer. Peter got thrown from the vehicle, and aside from a few contusions, survived the accident. Valerie wasn't so lucky. Dressed in a stunning dress, her hair teased and curled to perfection, life ended with a sudden jolt under the bent frame of a monster rig.

I could never shake the feeling that if I wouldn't have asked her to go to the lake, she'd still be alive today.

Now, years later, shivering in a world where people lost every trace of human kindness, I got that feeling once again, only this time the girl's name was Beth Andrews. If I hadn't said her name over the transmitter, she wouldn't be in the crosshairs of a madman.

Walking down the alley, I hung a sudden left on Chamberlain Drive towards Beth's house.

"You're crazy man. You're freaking crazy!" the voice inside my head shouted. *"You wanna die? Pack it up and go home before it's too late."*

Brushing away the thoughts, I gripped the baseball bat and hurried down Chamberlain.

Beth's house was only a few blocks away. Within minutes I found myself crouched behind a utility shed at the rear entrance. The wind moaned in a tall tree; its branches extended into the dark sky like the haunted arms of meatless corpses.

For an instant my courage evaporated into the cold night air. I wanted to run. Hightail it out of there and retreat back to the un-lush confines of my dirty cellar. I know. That doesn't sound brave. But these days being a hero only worked in the movies. Unlike the big screen, when people died here, they didn't come back.

Looking at the house, everything appeared quiet. Maybe the gunman was bluffing. I left out a sigh of relief, but just as quickly, the radio came back online.

"Hey Eddie, are you out there cowboy?"

"Right here." I swallowed hard.

"Did you bring the goods?"

Stuffing my hands in my pockets, I pulled out a half eaten candy bar. "First send the girl out."

"You really got me pegged as an idiot, don't you?" He laughed hard and then stopped cold. "Bring the food in the house," he ordered. "Come upstairs. Don't try any heroics. One slip and I'll cut her throat."

"How do I even know Beth is up there?"

"You doubt my veracity?"

"I think you're lying," I challenged.

"Where are you?"

"I'm outside, the back of the house."

"Perfect," he said. "Look up at the second floor, the window to the right."

Peeking out from behind the utility shed, I scanned the exterior of the second floor.

"I don't see anything."

"You're not very sharp-eyed, are you cowboy?" he said in a gravelly voice. "Look again."

I scanned the second floor. Finally my eyes bolted on a window to the right. A flashlight flicked on and illuminated a woman, her face shadowed in terror. The darkened silhouette of a man stood directly behind her. Grabbing her by a tuft of hair, he yanked her head backwards. The edge of a knife, glinting and sharp, probed her throat. Suddenly the flashlight went dark again.

I stood there wide eyed with a gaping mouth.

"Any more questions?" he asked smartly. "Now get your ass up here."

7

Guess who's coming to Dinner

Walls of dread crushed in all around me. The tiger readied itself to strike. It was true. He had been listening to every word I said on the radio. He found Beth, took her hostage, and now he wanted me.

I wanted to run but couldn't. If I did, there would be no stay of execution, and me? I'd be the person flipping the switch on the electric chair. Beth would die.

"You got yourself into this," said the little voice in my head. *"Remember what your old football coach used to tell you when you weren't warming the bench? Show some guts. If you want to score, don't give them room to breathe. Hit hard and fast."*

Isn't that the truth? I needed to beat him to the punch. Employ guerrilla warfare. Open fire and then get the hell out before he ever had a chance to recover from the blow.

Holding firm to the baseball bat, I quietly moved past a rusted swing set in Beth's yard, ducked behind a hedge and then ran up a pair of wooden steps that led the kitchen entrance. Taking a deep breath, I slipped inside.

It was dark. I had to risk switching on my flashlight even if it meant compromising my position. Looking around, the kitchen table had been overturned. Dishes were smashed on the linoleum floor.

Tip-toeing into the living room, a fireplace sat dormant against the back wall of the house. A picture of Beth with a little girl, eyes sparkling and standing next to a Ferris wheel, hung on the wall. A couple of music CD's and candles sat on a dusty coffee table dabbed with melted wax.

"Last chance," the desperate voice in my head said. *"Get out of there. Head for home before it's too late."*

I considered the proposal for a minute but a loud thump upstairs froze me to the carpet. My fingers slid tight around the bat. It was a formidable weapon but sure as hell it wouldn't stop a bullet. For all I knew, a red dot had already been painted on my forehead.

Firming up my courage, I walked to the bottom of the stairway and began to climb. One squeak of a floorboard would be enough to give me away.

Reaching the top of the stairs, I listened close. The silence was deafening. Once I heard a noise only to discover that it was the sound of my own heavy breathing.

Walking down the hall, I came to the first bedroom and shined my flashlight in the room. White cotton sheets with red hearts were pulled neatly up on the bed. Jewelry had been strewn around on top of a vanity. Otherwise, the room was unoccupied.

I continued down the hall. A pasty film of nervous sweat splashed over my forehead. I had no idea how to overpower my opponent but the directive was clear. I needed to be quick. Lightning fast. I'd have to storm the room, swing wildly and hope to connect with the opposition. After that? It was just a matter of getting back out again without taking a bullet to the head.

"You really got a death wish, don't you?" My subconscious again. The little bastard was working overtime. *"You should be running like a deer. In case you haven't heard, the hunter has you scoped. Once you step through that door there's no turning back."*

A few feet away from the last bedroom I heard rustling noises. The stink of stale whiskey hung in the air; no doubt the stench of my newfound friend.

"I know you're out there cowboy, close enough to spit," my adversary whispered from inside the room. "Remember. No tricks. You gonna come quietly or go out in a blaze of glory?"

"What do you think?" I held the baseball bat tight, my limbs pressed tight against the exterior wall of the room.

"I don't think you have the stomach for a fight." He let out a sinister laugh. "Come and prove me wrong." The crisp sound of a bullet being loaded in a gun chamber clapped the night. "Right now this is all business. Give me your supplies and the girl goes free. If you resist?" he said. "Things get personal. You got three seconds to decide."

I started to move but my feet froze as if lodged in a block of cement.

"Don't hesitate." The little voice in my head again. *"He knows you're scared and doesn't think you've got the guts for battle. Storm the place. Catch him off guard."*

Gritting my teeth, I leapt in the room and swung the bat wildly. Searching from corner to corner for a target, I didn't see anyone except a young woman curled up beside a bed.

"Beth, is that you?" I whispered.

And then it happened. Bang. Someone hit me from behind. The bat slid out of my hands. I crashed to the floor, my head bouncing off a corner bedpost. Groggy but still conscious, I looked up. A dark figure stood directly over me.

"I told you cowboy, no tricks." The cold barrel of his gun pressed against the side of my neck.

Straining to see, I finally got a glimpse of the man smiling grimly down on me.

"Frank?" I blinked in disbelief.

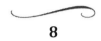

8

The Homecoming

I didn't see him since high school. His eyes looked criminally black; ink stains that with just a touch dirtied anything clean.

"Frank Myers?"

"Please." He laughed. "No applause, just throw money."

I remembered the guy all too well. Ever since school, his life had been the scum on a stagnant pool of water that polluted everything around him. You know the type, right? He was arrogant. Mean. Trouble. In school he loitered in halls and pounced on anyone too weak and unprotected to defend themselves. The last I heard, he got arrested in upstate New York when during a robbery at a convenience store, he bit off a cashier's ear.

Glancing over at Beth, she was down on her knees and leaning against a bedpost. Black electrical tape had been raveled over her mouth. Regardless of her inability to speak, every tense muscle of her body pleaded for help.

"What do you think Eddie?" Frank pulled a bottle of whiskey out of a filthy green jacket and took a slug. "We got ourselves a family reunion." Trudging over to Beth, he yanked her head back by the hair. "Isn't that right honey?"

"Let her go Frank." I stood up slowly.

"You really think you're in a position to be giving orders cowboy?" Frank asked.

I took a step forward.

Raising his weapon, he pointed it at my eye. "That's far enough."

Halting my advance, I asked, "I thought you were in jail?"

"I got a reprieve." Taking a last slug of whiskey, he stuffed the bottle back in his pocket. "Cops can be real animals, but every so often you get one with a heart. When the oil went south, so did law enforcement. Guards abandoned their posts. Some dumb ass warden unlocked my jail cell so I wouldn't starve to death. He said it was the humane thing to do. I'm telling you, he was one hell of a nice guy right up to the minute that I slit his throat and took his gun." He blew coolly on the barrel.

"I stayed in the city for awhile," Frank continued. "When the military arrived, they imposed curfews. The boys in uniform were anxious to put a bullet in anyone who stepped out of line. I decided to leave, hotwired a motorcycle, and headed back to the northeast, my old stomping grounds. Figured I'd stay here until things got under control. Like that will happen, right? We got a better chance of hitting the lottery while ice fishing in the Arctic."

For a guy contemplating murder, Frank was pretty damn chatty.

"It's only a matter of time until help comes," I told him.

"You're an ignorant bastard, aren't you?" He laughed loud. "This isn't like running out of toilet paper in the woods and grabbing a leaf off a tree. Look around. Compared to what's going on, a tsunami looks like a quick screw in the woods. People are rioting in the streets. It's Mardi Gras from Miami to Sacramento. Can't you smell it?" He sniffed. "Food is gone, water is scarce, and not even the frigid temperatures can hide the stench of dead bodies. Welcome to the dark ages, free to pillage and murder."

I had no idea if Frank told me the truth. Still he was right about one thing. Rules for survival in the world had changed. The sharp Maserati parked outside of the First National was about as useful as a butter knife in a cage filled with alligators. When the oil famine hit, civilization fell off the cliff. There were no more cops out on patrol or eating jelly donuts at the local convenience stores. The torch had been passed to those select individuals who had the biggest guns and the guts to open fire.

"How did you find me?" I asked.

"Dumb luck. When I got back to town, I made camp in the bar at The Mahoning Motel. Let me tell you, before I got incarcerated, I had some good drinking memories in that place. Scored with all of the ladies," Frank boasted. "The place was deserted but I found a few bottles of the hard stuff in the stock room. Figured I'd stick around and drink up the profits.

"While I was looking around I found this stupid radio stuffed under a counter in the lobby. The damn thing still worked. When I turned it on, you were on the frequency spouting off about all the food you had. After you mentioned Beth's name, I paid her a visit. Figured if she got in trouble, you'd come to the rescue. That's how love is, right? Guys always want to be a hero."

I stared at Frank, eye to eye. He was crazy, and crazy people were dangerous. I didn't have a bachelor's degree in psychology, but I wasn't stupid. Giving him food wouldn't solve any problems. Once he had what he wanted, he'd kill me anyway.

"I can get you everything you want." I tried stalling. "Give me some time."

"Time?" Frank raised an eyebrow. "I got lots of that. What I need is food, supplies."

"Frank..."

"Enough talk." He cut me off. Raising the gun, he pressed the barrel against Beth's neck.

"No!" I stepped forward.

"Easy," Frank warned. "Don't get brave. Didn't you ever go to the movies? Heroes die every day."

Stopping cold, my fingernails dug into the palms of my hands.

"That's smart," he said. "No sense getting bloodstains on the carpet."

I tried to anticipate Frank's next move, but what did I know about the criminal mind? Gazing into his eyes was like falling into a black and waterless hole where nothing lived. He was part of the new world order, born without oil and raised in chaos.

And me? I was an unemployed car salesman. A big Saturday night included dinner at the Chinatown Buffet and a Tom Cruise movie. That, of course, had changed. These days everyone lived on death row; it was just a question of time before we all walked the last mile.

I shifted my gaze to Beth. If I was scared, she looked petrified. Gagged with electrical tape and struggling to breathe through her nose, fear crawled on her face like ticks on a dead fawn. Dark shadows hung in her eyes, not from sleeplessness or moonlight filtering in the window, but rather the realization of dread that arrived in the form of one Frank Myers.

"On the radio you said that you have food." Frank jostled the trigger of his gun and tapped a heavy boot on the carpet. "Give it to me. If you do, nobody gets hurt."

"Why should I believe you?"

"Like there's a choice?" He pulled Beth up by the hair, the gun riding dangerously against her cheek.

"Take it easy." I raised my hands.

"The food, Eddie. Give me the food."

"There's some in my pocket."

"Put it on the bed."

"I don't have much."

"Give me the food."

"But..."

"Put the fucking food on the bed!" Frank shouted angrily and stuck the gun in the gully of Beth's eye.

Chills pricked my spine as I looked into Beth's frightened eyes.

Let me tell you something. People think they know about life. Get it straight. You don't know anything until you're confronted with a killer and looking down the wrong end of a loaded gun barrel.

My breath quickened. Every hair on my head tingled and my heart fluttered like the thrumming wings of a caged bird. Terror, a circling raven, swept in. In a world where stale bread and bottled water were sufficient reasons to kill someone, I wanted little to do with what life had become. Still, confronted with the prospects of being gunned down, a naïve deer in the woods, I wanted to live.

"I'll get the stuff," I told him. Slowly reaching in my pocket, I pulled out a half eaten candy bar and a bottle of Fiji water. "Take this for now. Think of it as a down payment." Leaning over, I tossed the foodstuff on the bed.

"That's it?" Frank blinked. "On the radio you shot off about having lots of food and supplies."

"I can get more." I kept my hands in the air and eyed the baseball bat on the floor.

"How much more?"

"I got rations stashed away. Mostly canned food and MRE's."

Frank's expression darkened. What the hell was he expecting, a turkey dinner with all the trimmings? Finding a soup bone gnawed on by a starved dog was impossible, let alone a full course meal.

Pockmarked with anger, Frank stormed over and struck me in the stomach with the handle of the gun. I crumpled to the carpet. "You think I went through all of this for a candy bar?"

Glaring with contempt, Frank turned around and walked back over to Beth. Holding the weapon on her, he squeezed the woman's throat. Beth gasped for air. "You're making me angry cowboy. Trust me. You don't want to see me angry," he said. "You broke your promise Eddie. You said you had food. You know what convicts do when someone breaks a promise?" He shook Beth like a dusty mop, her eyes filled with fright.

"I can get you supplies," I begged him. "I can get..."

"Shut up and listen," he ordered. "I'd hate to see something bad happen here." He kept the gun tight against Beth's cheek. "You wouldn't want that on your conscience. But I will Eddie. I'll kill her, right here, right now, unless you give me what I want."

"Leave her go Frank."

"Last chance. Give up the goods."

"I already told you, I need time. I'll get them for you."

"You want me to believe that?" Staring through half-lidded eyes, Frank pulled the whiskey back out, took another slug and tossed the empty bottle on the floor. "Nobody has to suffer here, least of all your little tramp. But you?" He snorted doubtfully. "You don't even have the guts to stop me, do you?" Reaching down, he jerked Beth's head back exposing her throat, ripe for cutting.

The tape suddenly loosened on her mouth and she let out a horrific scream.

Suddenly I heard a branch break; at least that's what it sounded like to me. Something snapped. Primitive thoughts, vultures in flight, circled in my head. Rivers of fear turned into an ocean of rage. I wanted to crush Frank and make him bleed. Nothing else mattered.

Springing to my feet, I lunged for the baseball bat and grabbed it off the floor. Frank whirled around, took aim and squeezed off a round. The bullet veered left in the wall and I swung the bat hard, hitting his arm. The blow was enough to make him lose his grip and drop the weapon.

Moving in quickly, I struck again. Frank raised his hands and grabbed the tip of the bat. Pulling it out of my hands, he flung it across the room. It smashed into a lamp that crashed on the floor. Still I wasn't finished. My bony fist crunched into Frank's nose, drawing blood.

The thing is, my profession was selling cars and drinking caffeinated coffee with perspective customers, not beating up hardened criminals. That wasn't much of a resume when pitted against a killer loose from his restraints.

Frank rammed a knee in my ribs. I groaned and buckled. Even drunk, he was agile as a cat. Scooping the gun off the floor, he put me in the crosshairs and stared with fierce intensity.

"You just had to be a hero, right cowboy?" Frank's finger jostled the trigger.

Standing there in the line of fire, decidedly a person's life really does flash before their eyes when the journey ends. I found myself drifting back in time before the world spun out of control. I wasn't Einstein but had a promising career at the car dealership. If nothing else, I looked pretty spiffy in a pair of kakis and polished shoes. I thought about things, stupid things, like punching numbers in an ATM machine or ordering takeout pizza from Kleintop's. I thought about other things too, including watching a sunrise over the ocean from a boardwalk balcony and a crush I had on a summer camp councilor when I was a kid. I thought about all those things and the good memories of my life.

The problem was, those same good memories were now far-off echoes in a distant canyon. That kid sporting pimple cream with the geeky haircut no longer existed. When the oil shortage slammed me in the face, I fell through a crack and landed in a ghetto. Tired and hungry, I was forced to turn into a reluctant warrior on this battlefield called earth.

"You gonna kill me Frank?" I turned suddenly courageous. I don't know why. Maybe I just gave up on life. At times it seemed as if dying would be the easier course. Still I wasn't giving Frank any room to gloat. "Pull the trigger. That's the plan, isn't it?"

Confusion washed over Frank. His lips, thin and wiry, trembled with an underbelly of anger. He didn't like defiance. Even more, he detested being challenged.

"You don't understand." He stared me down. "I get it. You don't care about your own life, but what about someone else?" He shifted his attention to Beth. "You hear that darlin'? It's official. Your boyfriend made you the sacrificial lamb. If I remember right, in school you always wanted to be a dancer on Broadway. Sorry. That one isn't gonna happen." He aimed the weapon in her direction. "Say goodbye to Hollywood."

Beth's eyes grew threefold as she gazed into the sights of the killer.

"Frank!" I shouted. "Stop!"

A grim smile painting his lips, Frank pulled the trigger. The shot boomed in the dry tunnels of night.

"See you in the next life." Blowing on the gun's barrel, he disappeared out the door.

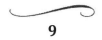

9

Rescue Me

Beth's head slumped to one side and her arms went limp. Crawling over, I kneeled down beside her.

"Can you hear me?" I touched her arm. "Beth?"

Curtains flapped in an icy breeze from a broken window. Beth didn't move, and darkness, deeper than a mineshaft, crushed in all around me.

I sat there and stared at the ashes of a girl who I once fell in love with back in high school. But there were no more friendly little towns where young lovers parked by lakesides in convertibles and watched the shooting stars. Life had become a theatre of war.

Cradling Beth's head in my hands, I looked up and caught sight of my reflection in a mirror. That guy in the dapper shirt and red tie that traipsed around an automobile showroom had vanished. Gone was the stylish London Fog coat in lieu of a filthy green jacket insulated with duck quilt, stolen from a neighbor's house. Thin and dirty, I had become that homeless person in the streets, begging for pennies and shunned by people who drove expensive cars and lived in glass houses. These days the oil famine leveled the playing field for everyone. I suppose that's poetic justice; now we all lived under bridges and knew the meaning of destitute and losing.

Turning my attention back to Beth, her quiet face stared at the bedroom ceiling. It occurred to me that if the cruel world didn't eradicate the innocent, people like Frank Myers would.

"Beth?"

The only sound heard was the haunting flap of the broken screen door and the rustle of wind outside.

A glacier of anger gushed over me. Gently placing Beth's head on the floor, I stood up, picked up the wooden bat and went to the bedroom window.

"Frank!" I shouted and smashed the bat against the wall, shattering a picture. "Show yourself!"

Looking out into the dark tunnels of night, everything remained secretive and unfamiliar. From the churches to the jails, danger painted every dark corner. Without so much as a streetlight and nomads like Frank running loose, I stood in unfamiliar terrain, and for all practical purposes, might as well have been living on Mars.

My thoughts were abruptly diverted when I heard a voice murmur, "Eddie."

Turning around, I dropped the bat and quickly raced back to Beth.

Beth's eyes blinked open. I reached out to touch her arm but she pulled back as if a tarantula crawled up her sleeve.

"Take it easy." I raised my hands and backed off. "Frank is gone."

Her head turned from side to side and her face was chiseled into a block of fear. She wearily traced her hands over her blouse and searched for an entry wound.

I looked her over. It didn't make sense and bordered on a miracle. Frank fired from no more than a few feet away, but other than a smudge of grime on her shirt, there were no injuries and certainly nothing that would justify being shot at point blank range.

"You must have an angel on your shoulder. I don't see anything." I looked again for any bloodstains. "Frank missed."

Beth's eyes swelled with fear at the mention of his name. "What if he comes back?"

"We're not gonna be around long enough to find out," I told her.

A loud noise downstairs made me fear the worst, but it was just the wind banging a door off the rear of the house.

Looking around the room, I asked, "Are you alone?"

"What do you mean?" She stared at me.

"I saw a picture hanging on the wall downstairs. You were with a little girl, standing by a Ferris wheel. You have a daughter," I said. "Is she here?"

"Ashley," she said.

"What?"

"My daughter," said Beth. "Her name is Ashley. Just before the oil disaster, she went to visit my sister in Rockport. I tried to call her but all the power went out. I have no idea if she's even alive."

"I'm sure she's okay." I touched Beth's hair.

She folded her head in her hands and then looked up at me through damp eyes. "How did all of this happen to us?"

Guilt weighted my shoulders down and my head drooped to the floor. If I wouldn't have mentioned Beth's name on the radio, Frank wouldn't have found her.

Another bang at the kitchen screen door hastened my resolve to get moving. Helping Beth up, we hurried out of the house.

A light snow began to fall and glistened off trees and housetops. Every street was quiet and desolate, almost as if time had stopped.

Silent as cats, we trudged up the alleyway towards my house. Perspiration dampening her skin and dark hair falling in her face, Beth stumbled forward.

"It's almost the holiday," she said.

"What?"

She stopped walking and turned towards me. "It'll be Christmas in a few days."

I blinked uncertainly. "I almost forgot."

Thinking about it, I could still see those blustery winter nights when I was young. Windows sparkled with lighted trees and shiny ornaments. People caroled on street corners and drank hot cocoa. Looking around, things had changed. Instead of the Bach and Handel Choir singing Silent Night, gunshots reverberated off the tenements, and predators, poised to strike, hid in the shadows of hedges.

Beth had trouble keeping up the pace. A blanket of exhaustion covered her. She stopped a few times and bent down, hands on knees, almost as if unable to take another step.

"I don't know if I can go on." Breathing hard, she coughed.

Let me tell you something. I'm not one of those macho guys who live inside a gym. The most exercise I got was bending an elbow over a few beers at The Molly's on a Saturday night. Still I'd be damned if I'd let Beth give up. Tucking an arm around her waist, I helped her walk as we trudged into the darkness.

When we finally reached the house, Beth sat down in the frozen grass, out of breath.

"Wait here," I told her.

I shimmied through the crawlspace that led into the cellar of the house and removed the boards that were nailed into the backdoor, and then brought Beth inside. Pulling out a kerosene heater that kept the pipes from freezing in the winter, I lit it up. It wasn't Cabo Wabu or a luxurious island resort in the Caribbean but at least it beat the arctic chill filtering in from Canada.

Beth sat in front of the kerosene heater with a blanket thrown over her shoulders. She was a beautiful woman with eyes softer than summer rain. Still her skin looked pale and she repeatedly coughed. A month ago I would have driven her over to Doc Thomas's office for a checkup, but these days? Physicians left town and hospitals closed. The closest thing to good healthcare was shredded bed linen to use as a tourniquet.

"You don't sound good." I handed her a bottle of water.

"I'll live." She drank and started coughing again. "I have a respiratory infection. I've been taking amoxicillin but the pills are gone. I guess it's too late to get that last refill at the drugstore." She forced a halfhearted smile.

"Don't worry," I worried. "Help should get here soon. They'll bring supplies."

Beth didn't answer, nor did she believe it. I didn't believe it either. Given a planet where the entire human race needed rescuing, chances that the National Guard would slog across the snow and ice in the near future were at best, bleak. We were on our own.

"I know where there might be some medicine," I finally said.

Beth's frightened eyes blinked. "You can't go out there. It's dangerous. Besides, what if Frank knows we're here? I can't fight him off alone."

"If he didn't come so far, we're probably safe." I answered but didn't sound convinced.

Beth coughed again. There was a deep rattle that started up in her chest. My mother used to call it a death rattle; that terrible sound when someone approaches their last breath. Beth wasn't at that point. I intended to make sure it stayed that way.

"If you don't get medicine, you'll get worse." I touched her hand and paused. "I might know a place to find some. I could be back within the hour."

Beth looked up at me with somber eyes. Leaning on her elbows, she kissed my cheek. The soft glow of the kerosene heater glimmered on her face. She cuddled her head on a pillow against my shoulder. I didn't move, not a muscle. After awhile she closed her eyes.

Quietly getting up, with one last look I headed back into the darkness.

10

Jimmy Stokes

Some years ago I worked the graveyard shift in the steel mills with a guy named Jimmy Stokes. We operated the blast furnaces. I swear you'd sweat ten pounds off your hips before the final buzzer rang each morning.

Jimmy, a bird-like man with an overbite, was a hypochondriac. He had so many pharmaceuticals stocked away in his house you'd have thought he was employed by a Mexican drug lord.

"I saw a report last night on the news about colon cancer," he confided in me one day. Sucking nervously at his lip, he said, "Do you think I might have that one?"

Stepping away from the furnace, I wiped my forehead with a dirty towel. "What makes you think that?"

"The guy on the news said it's a silent killer."

"Microwaves give off radiation," I reminded him. "Preservatives in food aren't a bargain either. I don't hear you complaining about that."

"Microwaves?" Jimmy blinked.

"Forget I said that."

But Jimmy wouldn't forget it. In fact thoughts of it kept him up all night. The following morning he unplugged the microwave, tied it up in cardboard and put it outside for trash night. He also cleaned out his refrigerator. Preservatives were on the hit list, including ammonium sulfate, sodium nitrite, titanium dioxide and about ten other words I couldn't even begin to pronounce.

Later that afternoon Jimmy drove to the emergency room at the hospital. Before the receptionist could talk, he slammed his fist on the front desk and demanded that a doctor perform emergency surgery for colon cancer.

"Calm down sir," the receptionist told him. "What are your symptoms?" she inquired.

"Symptoms?" Jimmy was caught off guard. "What the hell kind of a question is that? I'm a taxpayer and I'm telling you, I need an operation."

Jimmy Stokes never got a cancer operation but he did get increasingly worse with paranoia over the years. If a new virus turned up on the news, he became instantaneously susceptible to the threat. Penicillin, amoxicillin, and even a voodoo remedy from a boardwalk gypsy that he got on vacation two years ago to ward off Ebola, were stuffed in his cupboard.

I hadn't seen much of Jimmy since the days at the steel mills. Still, with most or all medical facilities closed, he was my best hope when it came to finding medicine.

Jimmy's house looked deserted. I knocked but nobody answered. Turning the knob, the door wasn't locked so I walked in.

"Jimmy?" I scanned the room. "Hey man, are you here? It's Eddie Slate."

Looking around, old newspapers were stacked up on the kitchen counter. The sink overflowed with dishes and scrunched up Budweiser cans littered the trashcan. Still there were no signs of Jimmy.

Stepping over to the countertop, I scoured through some cabinets above the refrigerator. I found an empty aspirin bottle and a pair of musty reading glasses, but nothing of value.

Scratching at beard stubble, it occurred to me that if Jimmy had pills stashed in the house, they'd be in a safe place, maybe a closet or stuffed in the back of a drawer in the bathroom. I turned towards a flight of stairs to make my way to the second floor but stopped cold. A shadow stood in a darkened corner of the room. I knew the face. Jimmy Stokes stared at me. A monstrous German Sheppard stood rigid at his side.

"Move and you're dead," he said in a threatening tone. Picking a carving knife up off the kitchen counter, he held it tight in his fist.

I backed up a step and raised my hands. "Take it easy Jimmy. Remember me? It's Eddie Slate. We worked together at the steel mill. Those were the days, right?"

Jimmy's expression remained flat as a rock. "What do you want?"

"I got problems."

"Take a look around. We all do." He stared and tapped his foot impatiently. Pulling a handkerchief out of his pocket, he repeatedly wiped at his nose as if warding off unseen germs filtering in the air. "What are you doing in my house?"

I took a step forward but a throaty growl from the German Sheppard halted my advance. "I'm gonna give it to you straight Jimmy. I have a sick friend. Beth Andrews. She got a bad cough. Respiratory problems. I thought you might have something to help."

"What if I do?" Lightening up a little, Jimmy pulled a lighter out of his pocket and lit a candle on the stove.

"Just figured you might help out an old friend."

"I got no friends, least of all human ones." Reaching down, he scratched the dog behind the ears.

Glancing around, the house looked deserted. "Anyone else here?" I asked. "Things are tough these days. Nobody should be alone."

"But I am alone!" He angrily shoved the toaster off the countertop and it smashed on the linoleum.

Judging by the dark circles under Jimmy's eyes, he hadn't slept in days. I looked around the room again. "Where's your wife?"

Jimmy paused and then his expression wilted in the shimmer of candlelight. Finally he tossed both the carving knife and the handkerchief on the table. "Meg had heart surgery a few months back. She seemed okay but then the oil famine hit. The electric went off. It got cold. After awhile, she got feverish. The hospitals and emergency rooms were closed. I couldn't do much more than keep her warm with blankets, that and give her whatever medicine I had stashed, but nothing helped." He stared at the floor and sniffed back a tear.

"Damn Jimmy, I'm sorry to hear that," I told him.

He motioned towards the kitchen window and the backyard. "I buried her out there three days ago."

Looking at his tortured eyes, I didn't know what to say. Much like the rest of the planet, everything he had ever known and loved was gone.

After a minute Jimmy walked to the corner of the room, bent down and pulled up a loose floorboard. Sticking his hand in the hole, he pulled out a couple of pill bottles. "I keep this in case of emergencies. Barbs, amoxicillin, you name it." He tossed the pills on the counter next to the sink. "Take it all," he told me. "Nothing much matters anymore."

Reaching over slowly, I picked up the meds and shoved them in my pocket. Jimmy's shoulders slumped and his arms hung at his sides. His downcast eyes stared listlessly at a sofa in the living room, probably the one where his wife watched television at night. I'm not a soft touch, but honest to God, my heart cracked in three pieces when I saw him look to the window leading into the yard where he buried his wife in the snow.

"Do you have enough food?" I asked.

"I'll get by," he answered.

"Maybe you could come with me."

"And do what?" He laughed unenthusiastically. "Wait for the government to save us? I don't think so. Right now most of the politicians are holed up in some underground hotel, sizzling steaks and turning up the thermostat. Maybe the feds even wanted this to happen. You know, disposal of the weak and feeble. In case you didn't notice, that's us."

"That's crazy Jimmy," I told him. "The government wouldn't do this on purpose."

"Wouldn't they?" he said. "You ever see tramps living in cardboard boxes and under bridges trying to keep the rain of their noses? We send food all over the world but don't have the decency to throw our own people a bone. Does that make any sense to you?" He picked up a picture of his wife from the kitchen table and stared at it. Finally he announced, "I'm not going anywhere. I'm gonna finish things right here Eddie. This is my home." He looked at the front door. "Take care of yourself."

"Things will get better," I said, uncertain of my own words. Turning to leave, I gave him a reassuring tap on the shoulder.

That's when the bullet came through the window and hit Jimmy Stokes' square in the temple.

11

The last American Desperado

Jimmy Stokes was dead before his head ever bounced off the linoleum floor.

Dread washed over me as I lunged and took cover under the kitchen table. The bullet left a gaping hole the size of a baseball in a window above the kitchen sink.

The German Sheppard quickly lumbered over beside its master. Letting out a threatening growl, the animal barked as if to ward off approaching enemies.

Looking around, the exit door of the house stood only a few feet away. But judging by the puncture wound in Jimmy Stokes' head, I wouldn't make it three steps before the sniper zeroed in on me.

A noise from my pocket diverted my attention.

"Hey Eddie, you there man?"

I pulled the radio out.

"Frank?" I tilted my head.

Another bullet shattered the window. This one landed in the refrigerator with a dull thud, only inches away from my face.

"No sense hiding," said Frank. "I was a crack shot in the army."

"You killed Jimmy Stokes," I said angrily.

"Desperate times warrant extreme measures."

"What do you want from me?"

"You told me you had food Eddie. You didn't deliver the goods."

I curled up tight under the table. My eyes were cemented on the exit door. "I already told you, I can get more food. I just need time."

"You don't understand," said Frank. "This isn't about a box of cornflakes. You lied to me Eddie. It's personal now."

I looked at Jimmy Stokes. His head smudged against the floor, a runner of blood dripped on the linoleum. If Frank had his way, I'd be joining him.

"After our little get together at Beth's house, I circled around the block and came back to finish things but the both of you were gone," said Frank. "Unless you hauled her corpse down the street, the bullet must have strayed off target. She doesn't know how lucky she is. I'm a perfect shot, the last of the great American desperados. You can bet your ass I won't miss again."

"Why can't you just leave us alone?" I shivered, staring from the window to the door.

"Calm down cowboy. You're a walking coronary. Your buddy on the floor won't ever have to worry about that one, right?"

I glanced at Jimmy. His lifeless eyes stared at the ceiling. "You murdered him."

"Who am I to argue?" Frank's voice was alive with pleasure. "What you should know is this. I'm gonna do the same damn thing to you Eddie, not to mention the girl, what's her name again, Beth?"

"Don't touch her!" I gripped the radio.

"Do yourself a favor," he advised. "Forget women. They're trouble. Most of them lie more than a whore on Bourbon Street." Another bullet whizzed past my ear and buried itself in the corner of the kitchen table. "Enough talk. So what's it gonna be cowboy? A quick shot to the head that'll drop you faster than a rock, or do I take out your kneecaps and leave you lying on the carpet for the rats to finish the job?"

I stared at the exit. Frank had an impeccable aim, still I'd have to risk running. If I didn't, he'd kill me quick.

"I'm a fair guy Eddie," said Frank. "Just because I'm an ex-con doesn't make me a monster. It's true," he admitted. "There's a dark angel on your head; you're scoped. Can you feel it?"

A cold shiver ran down my extremities.

"I'll tell you what. I'm gonna count to five. Here's the deal. If you run, I'll open fire. You'll be a moving target so I can't guarantee a clean shot. You could suffer," Frank admitted.

"On the other side of the coin," he continued, "stay where you are and I'll make it a dirt free shot, directly through the skull. It'll be painless. Quick. You make the call. You've got until the count of five. One..." he counted off.

I glanced around the kitchen and at the flight of stairs in the next room. I could run up to the second floor of the house. But even if I made it that far, Frank would come after me. There'd be no way back downstairs and out of the house. I'd be trapped.

"Two."

The carving knife on Jimmy Stokes' kitchen table was within arm's length. I could grab it but Frank had a gun. He'd cut me down before I ever got close enough to strike.

"Three."

My heart pounded. The only viable means of escape was a door on the other side of the kitchen. It led to a garage in the basement, the problem being, even if I made it outside, I'd be an open target in the streets.

"Four." Frank accented the word as if he were a golfer ready to hit a ball.

Mountains of uncertainty poured over me, but this wasn't the time for indecision. Run or die; it was just that simple. I'd have to move quickly, rabbit fast.

"Five!" Frank shouted loudly.

I bolted off the kitchen floor. A bullet shattered another windowpane. It landed less than a foot away in a cabinet. Taking flight, I ran towards the steps that led to the garage and hurried down them. For an instant I thought I might have bested him. Then my shoe got collared in a wooden step. I lost my balance and tumbled down the staircase. My head banged off the floorboards at the bottom.

Shaking the mist from my vision, I looked up and saw Frank staring down on me. Toting a rifle, he shined a flashlight in my eyes. Upstairs, Jimmy Stokes' dog lingered over his master's body and growled fiercely at the commotion.

"Shut up or you'll be next!" Frank hollered up the steps.

Turning his attention back to me, Frank said, "You screwed with me Eddie. You didn't come through on your end of the bargain." He raised a heavy boot and dropped it on my gut. The wind jammed from my lungs. "I don't like being played. How am I supposed to forgive something like that?" The stench of whiskey reeked from his pores.

"You gonna kill me Frank?" Glaring, I refused to back down.

Frank laughed in a rough voice. "I wouldn't want to disappoint you." He shoved the gun barrel under my chin. Smiling grimly he squeezed the trigger. Nothing happened but an empty click.

I let out a sigh of relief.

"Scared you, didn't I?" Frank grinned. "I'm out of ammo, not that it matters."

Sliding a knife out from underneath his belt, he twirled it in his fingers then leaned down and rested it tight against my throat. "I could finish things, right here, but I won't," said

Frank, probing my neckline with the blade. "Today I'm gonna give you a free pass cowboy." Shoving the knife back under his belt, he stood up and took a step back. "The thing is I'm not sure I can guarantee that passage of safety for Beth."

"Leave her go Frank," I leaned up on my elbows. "This is between you and me."

Raising his boot, he kicked me in the face. Blood trickled from my nose. "Don't interrupt me again," he warned. "Tell me something. You ever go fishing Eddie?" I stared but said nothing. "When my old man wasn't piss drunk, he used to take me to the Packer Dam. We'd fish for catfish. Gut them just right the innards spill out like a cold can of worms. That's how I see your girlfriend. She's one nice catch. Women like that go for guys like me. They're attracted to the bad element. I'd give her something to moan about Eddie, you know what I'm saying? I want you to think about that while you're out on the tiles. Think about it hard."

"Leave her alone!" I shouted again, struggling to get up.

Frank smirked. "Pleasant dreams." Raising his weapon, he dropped the handle down hard on my forehead. A second later, everything turned black.

12

My Shadow

I blacked out, perhaps for minutes, maybe hours. When I finally woke up, the silhouette of a large rat sat on the ledge of a musty window. At first I was confused as to my whereabouts. Fingering the back of my neck, tender to the touch, I quickly remembered. Frank shot Jimmy Stokes and then clubbed me on the head.

When I tried to stand, it didn't take long to figure out that I had more wounds to contend with. A sharp pain cut through my lower extremities. Upon falling down the stairs, a sliver of wood pierced my ankle. It wasn't much bigger than a pencil but might as well have been a Samurai sword. When I yanked it out the poachers probably heard me scream all the way down on Park Street.

Craning my head to see inside the kitchen at the top of the stairs, the candle still burned on the stove. I could just barely see the tips of Jimmy Stokes' boots as he lay on the floor. The dog sat at attention beside him, panting hard.

"Come here boy." I whistled.

The Sheppard never flinched and refused to leave his post. Intent on safeguarding his master, the dog would fight, die if need be, to have its loyalty proven.

Turning around, I hobbled out the door and into the street.

The traffic lights were dark and the town clock, fixed at 1:11 a.m. forever, made me shudder. I couldn't help feeling as if I were in a dream where the entire world suddenly stopped.

There were still no signs of Frank. Then again I didn't expect to find him curled up behind a hedge zeroing in on me. If he wanted me dead, he would have finished the job already.

I walked down the road and stopped in front of Saint Mark's church. An old woman with grey hair, bundled in a heavy coat, kneeled down in the courtyard. She barely moved and for a minute I thought that she might have succumbed to the cold.

"Are you okay?" I asked.

The woman turned to look. Lowering her head again, she folded her hands in a silent prayer.

Further down the road, a lopsided CLOSED sign hung on the door of Duran's coffee shop. I could hear a man and woman arguing on the second floor of the building. In the new world, standard disputes would no longer be about how to pay the rent or taxes. Breadwinners in a post oil free planet hinged on rummaging through trashcans for food and looting a neighbor's house.

Stopping in the middle of the street, I listened to the silence. There were no church bells, no music, and no children's laughter in the playground. The only sound was that of a distant scream and a gunshot. I couldn't help but to wonder what happened to the hope of rescue, that white stallion that gallops over the mountainside carrying a brave rider. Where was the promise of a good life that with every passing day faded into colors of autumn, swept away in the wind and shadowed in the dark corners of this new and fearsome world? Staring into the streets, the gutters littered with garbage moving in cold wind, I had to ask myself, "How did we let it all happen?"

A few doors down from Milo's Gas Station, I again had the disturbing sensation of being watched. At first I thought it might be my imagination, but I heard noises. Something moved.

Turning around, I expected to find a vagrant pointing a rifle or wielding a knife. Instead of a ruthless killer, a familiar face came into view.

Jimmy Stokes' dog trailed me. The animal looked on with sad eyes. Wagging its tail, it left out a sneeze and then shyly lowered its head.

I stiffened. The animal was big. If it turned on me, the fight would be faster than throwing a firecracker at a loaded Uzi.

"Hey boy." I whistled and held out my hand.

Making a slow approach, the dog nuzzled its head against my leg. Reaching down slowly, I patted it on the head and checked the tags on his collar.

"So your name is Shadow." I scratched him behind the ears.

Shadow made a slight whine and again cuddled against me.

"Okay then," I said. "Join the party."

Looking suspiciously up and down the street, there were still no signs of Frank. That didn't surprise me. He had other itineraries, one that included Beth, and if he found her?

Picking up the pace, I crossed the street down on 5th towards Center. Shadow followed close behind.

By the time I got back to the house, my ankle throbbed like a rotted tooth. Looking around the place from the backyard, it immediately struck me that something was amiss. When I left, the back door was closed. Now it hung wide open, flapping in the wind. Any flower of joy at my arrival quickly wilted as if in poisoned ground.

Someone was inside the house.

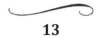

13

The Crawlspace

A sledgehammer of fear came down on my head. Dangerous people combed the night, but Frank was the real dread. If he found Beth, he'd hold firm to his threats.

"Looks like there's gonna be a duck shoot," said the rude voice in my head. *"I'll give you this; you might be stupid, but you got guts. If there's a shooter in there, you'll be dead before you ever walk two feet inside the place."*

Point taken. I decided to use the crawlspace as a means of entry into the house. If an intruder was inside, entering through the front door would make me an open target.

"Shadow." I scratched the dog behind the ears. "Stay here, understand?"

Wagging a long tail and sniffing, the dog settled back on its haunches.

Dragging a tender ankle, I slipped inside the access window of my house.

The crawlspace, black as night, was a haunt for spiders. I couldn't afford even a loud breath. If Frank or some other unknown attacker heard me coming, I'd be rat food for the duration of a long cold winter.

CRUDE

Crawling on all fours in dead silence, I couldn't help but to look back and wonder about things. Nobody could have imagined this thirty days ago. My idea of a rough night was getting stuck at the dealership after 5:30 on a Friday with an ornery customer trying to get a free oil change on a car deal. That's a long way from shimmying underneath the kitchen floor to confront an enemy, motives unknown.

Inching along, finally I reached the opening that led into the cellar. I could just barely see the red glow of the kerosene heater. It cast an eerie shadow over stone walls.

"Beth?" I risked a whisper.

There was no answer.

"*You're a lunatic?*" The little guy in my subconscious jumped in again. "*That's it, isn't it? You're certifiably crazy. Who knows what's waiting for you in there. Everyone out of the way!*" said the voice. "*Dead man walking.*"

Indecision knocked me around. I wanted to reverse motion, put her in reverse and creep out the same way I entered. Maybe I'd steal a bicycle from Hagar's yard, peddle my way to Daytona and camp on a warm beach. Still my conscience wouldn't allow it. Beth was in trouble. If Frank had her tied up inside, she'd be dead before sunrise.

"*If you're gonna do something dumb ass, you need to be quick,*" the little guy in my head announced. "*Get in the cellar, scan for enemies and subdue any impending threats, all inside a few seconds. That's a pretty tall order for a second rate car salesman.*"

Digging in the dirt, I found a loose rock. It wasn't a Smith & Wesson but at least it had some weight and would provide a means of defense.

"*Go for it, you crazy bastard!*" with one last blast the little guy in my head shouted.

Holding my breath, I lunged forward through the opening that led into the cellar. Landing on the floor, I rolled once and regardless of a bad ankle, sprung to my feet.

Beth huddled in the corner of the room. Her lily white face stared at me with a haunted expression.

"Are you alright?" I asked.

Beth's gaze shifted towards the stairs. A loud noise sounded out from the first floor. Theories of intruders suddenly turned to facts. Someone had entered the house.

The thud of a table or chair being toppled over made me cringe. A patter of footsteps on creaky floorboards moved towards the top of the cellar steps. The intruder knew we were here. As if to taunt us, the perpetrator even knocked his knuckles on the plaster walls.

Gripping the rock in my hand, I raised it in the air and readied myself to strike.

"This is what it all comes down to," the voice in my head said. *"It's time to separate the men from the killers."*

The step creaked at the top of the cellar and the intruder's sunken shadow, a malignant spirit roaming the night, silently looked down into the darkened room.

"Who the hell is up there?" I gripped the rock tight. "I'm warning you. Go away!"

My tough stance took an abrupt turn. I heard the sound of a gun hammer being pulled back. A rifle jammed tight against my neckline.

"Don't move," someone said. "Drop the rock."

I froze up.

"I said drop it," the assailant repeated.

The rock slid from my fingers and fell to the floor. With the weapon hugging the nape of my neck, I turned to look and blinked.

"Beth?"

14

Weapons of Love

You'd think that after thirty days of surviving in the trenches I'd have learned how to handle a crisis. Not so. Then again it'd be safer tucked in a sleeping bag in the middle of the Amazon jungle than walking down any street in America and abroad.

Life had decayed into chaos and betrayal. That's not to say I'm an angel. Sure. I screwed over a few customers, convinced them to buy expensive cars or unwanted lemons rusting away in the lot. But most of the time I offered a fair handshake. People have done worse. These days I mostly slogged around in ice and mud or shivered in a dank cellar, waiting for help to arrive; it didn't. Now I'm faced with the prospects of a gun barrel riding my backside. I'm not sure what I did to deserve all this but the punishment doesn't seem to fit the crime.

"Beth?" My head reeled in confusion.

"I said don't move," she answered and peered up at the top of the cellar steps. "Frank?" she called. "All clear."

Heavy boots started down the steps. In the sunken glow of the kerosene heater and a burning candle, Frank appeared.

"We meet again cowboy." A slippery grin played over his lips. Still grasping a bottle of the hard stuff, he took a long swallow. Grabbing me by the shirt, he flung me across the room and slammed me against the back wall of the cellar.

Staring blankly at Beth I said, "You're with him?"

"I don't remember asking you to talk." Frank glared. His cold eyes heartless as a wolf in the wild, he pulled the rifle from Beth's hands and pointed it at me.

A few years back I had a friend named Leo Braggs. Every summer he took a jet to Vegas. He was one cool cucumber when it came to playing poker. He told me winning hinged on reading an opponent's expression. "Watch the eyes and body language," he said. "That's the real ace in the hole."

At the moment, I didn't have so much as a pair of deuces. If I wanted to win the game I'd need to out-guess my opponent.

Looking at Beth, I couldn't help thinking that people are chameleons; they change colors. Surroundings dictate the necessary camouflage to stay alive in a predatory world. That's what happened to Beth. She changed. The attractive teenage girl with the strawberry lipstick who I once kissed while sitting on a beach blanket, no longer existed. Somewhere in the middle of the disaster she fought to find a viable means of survival in an un-survivable world.

Enter Frank, a bad ass criminal groomed to endure a hostile environment. A guy like that wouldn't think twice about opening someone's skull with a tire iron. Frank was a bear trap in the woods, covered with leaves and ready to snap. If Beth expected him to take care of her, she'd be disappointed. Sooner or later she'd slow him down or maybe just piss him off for eating what little food was available. He'd dump her on the side of some barren interstate, road-kill for possums and birds.

The reality is Beth didn't view me as a reliable respirator with the necessary apparatus to keep her alive in an unsympathetic world. I was a car salesman, not a murderer. I had no more endurance for survival in the trenches than a wealthy CEO hitting golf balls at the country club on a Sunday afternoon. Even with all those deficits, I still found it hard to believe she'd couple up with Frank.

"Don't you know what a guy like this will do to you?" I stared at her.

"You heard me the first time. Shut up." Frank crunched his fists.

"He killed Jimmy Stokes!" The words blurted out.

Frank marched across the room and knuckled me in the gut. Curling up, I dropped on one knee. "You know damn well that you're the one who wasted him." He gave a sly wink. "You left him there to die on the kitchen floor."

"That's a lie!"

"Is it?" Frank reached in his pocket and pulled out a cigarette. Lighting up, he blew a smoke ring in the air. "Forget Stokes." He changed the subject. "We got other business. We're in an oil famine. Most people lost a few belt sizes since this began, but you?" He eyed me head to toe. "You're not Mr. Universe but you're looking pretty fit in a world where people are starving to death. Something tells me you're not on the Nutra-diet system."

"I already told you. I don't have anything." I stared back at Frank and held my ground.

"You want me to believe that?" Frank took another drag on his cigarette. "All the cops went south with the oil famine. There's a new marshal in town. That would be me," he reminded. "I'd suggest you conform to protocol. Nobody is coming to save you."

Frank was dumb as a rock but had a prophetic outlook. At the moment we had a better chance of sprouting wings and migrating to Florida than FEMA manning the dog sleds and riding into town to restore order. With the entire country in shambles, help wouldn't be arriving soon.

Back in '92 in an incident that spurned the LA riots, police officers were acquitted after clubbing a suspect named Rodney King who was involved in a high speed chase. The verdict sparked an orgy of violence. In the end, over fifty people got killed along with a billion dollars in damages. That was an isolated incident. The oil disaster, on the other hand, was worldwide.

Politically exempt bigwigs, their families and mistresses aside, everyone, everywhere, would suffer the stains and aftermath of the current crisis. The black plague of disaster would spread from city to city, state to state, country to country. Odds of some shitty little car salesman from northeastern Pennsylvania surviving the trauma was about as likely as a Nazi war criminal walking into a bagel shop in Tel Aviv where the patrons all packed semi-automatics. The future looked grim.

"Why don't you just kill me and get it over with?" I stared at Frank, tempting fate.

"It's not that simple." Frank tapped a scuffed boot against a support beam in the corner of the room. "These days everyone abandoned their houses and headed south. The only people left in the streets are looters and vagrants. Then came you," he said. "You stuck around Eddie. Hell, you're like the Alamo. Something must be keeping you here."

"What are you talking about? You're still here," I reminded.

"I intended to move on." Frank crossed his arms and leaned coolly against the wall. "The way I saw it, everyone who had anything of value was either dead or gone. Everyone that is, except for you. When you said over the radio that you had food, I figured I could work out a business arrangement with the girl to get the goods."

I turned to Beth. "You set me up?"

Beth's chin dipped to her chest. Her face splashed in pools of guilt.

"Women, huh? They're weapons of love." Frank sniffed. "You just can't trust them."

It was hard to believe. Unfaithfulness has many masks, and betrayal, not the least of them. That's what I felt in that desperate moment: treachery and betrayal.

"You got everything I have Frank." A granite block of hate sat on my shoulders. "Just leave."

"I can't do that one cowboy." Frank hooked a thumb in his belt. "For one thing I'm betting you're holding out. After you left your house, I followed you. My guess was that you'd lead me to some provisions. Instead you took a detour to Jimmy Stokes' house. I remember him from back in high school. He turned me in for robbing a concession stand after a football game. That won't happen again." He grinned.

I stared into Frank's soulless eyes. Hatred, heavy as a chunk of iron, weighed on my heart. I wanted to kill him. It was just a question of finding an unguarded moment.

"Enough talk," said Frank. He kicked a wheelbarrow over that sat in the corner of the room and walked towards me. "Give me your supplies. Cooperate and I'll disappear faster than Houdini. Nobody gets hurt."

No doubt the guy had me figured for an idiot. Frank gunned down Jimmy Stokes on the kitchen tiles for pure pleasure. If I gave him everything he wanted, I'd be next. At the very least, he'd break my legs and leave me bleeding on the floor; a winter's feed for rodents.

"How do I know you'll keep your word?" I asked.

"You don't, but the alternatives are pretty clear." Frank beamed like a shark, his stained molars green with corruption.

After a minute, I slowly stood up and pointed at the corner of the cellar. "Over there. Supplies are behind that stack of old magazines."

Keeping a watchful eye on me, he walked to the corner of the room. Buried underneath a rusty red toolbox and bundled up magazines, he pulled out a jar of peanut butter, rations from the army store and a few cans of vegetable soup.

"That's a good start," Frank said. "Where's the rest?"

"I already explained. There's nothing else here."

I'm a shitty liar. That probably sounds like a walking contradiction coming from a car salesman. Put me on an automobile lot with some rich parents sending their kid off to college, I'd have them signing for a new convertible within the hour. The difference here was I didn't have the upper hand or a position of control. Frank had the power and I was made of glass, ready to shatter.

The truth is I did have more food, not to mention a few gallons of kerosene. Some of it I had stashed under some loose floorboards in the upstairs bedroom. The rest was stocked away in a dark corner of the crawlspace. That secret would remain in the closet. Frank might kill me, but I didn't know when help would arrive and I'd be damned if I'd give him my last piece of bread.

I shifted my gaze back to Beth. Her expression remained blank as a mannequin. I don't know what happened to the girl I once knew. She even taught Sunday school and baked blueberry pies for the kids in the summer. Frozen in the aftermath of a post oil free world, her face now looked chilled as a glacier.

"Don't try to con a con. You're holding out." Propping the rifle against the rear wall of the cellar, Frank picked up a rusty pipe wrench from atop the toolbox and tapped it in the palm of his hand. I hated plumbing, and at the moment, I had the distinct sensation that I'd hate it all the more before everything was over.

For a minute I thought about Chuck Grimes, a friend of mine in Allentown. I swear that crazy bastard was born with a rifle in his hands. Every year he bagged a deer. After the kill he'd gut the spoils and then hoist the furry remains up on a sturdy line in the backyard. The way he cuddled that thing, you'd have sworn it was a prize watermelon at the county fair. He was a stickler for intimate details. He wanted neighbors to know how he stalked and scoped his prey, took a deep breath and then squeezed the trigger.

"BANG!" he'd tell the boys in the bar over a cold one. "Dead between the eyes."

For all you animal rights activists, there's your sign, a surefire way to distinguish the hunters from the killers. Hunters want to feed their families; killers are only interested in the slaughter. That was Frank. He had his own agenda when it came to murder. Shooting someone like Leo Giannetti at the record store or Jimmy Stokes next to a kitchen sink wasn't sufficiently entertaining. He needed that chiseled sensation in his fingers of a sharp knife hitting bone.

"Trust me." Frank slowly turned the wrench in his fingers. "There are worse ways to die than a gunshot. Do you get my meaning?"

I got it, alright.

"I already told you. I don't have anything," I said.

"Still playing games?" He took a step closer with the pipe wrench. "Don't make me do this."

Frank issued an ultimatum and he'd follow through, even if it killed me.

15

Scare Tactics

Streaks of fear painted Beth's appearance. It was the first tangible emotion she displayed since jamming a gun in the back of my neck. Frozen solid, she stared at the pipe wrench locked in Frank's fist. Not only would he kill me, he wouldn't hesitate to cancel Beth's breathing habits if he perceived her as a threat.

Frank paced the floor. He stopped abruptly in front of me and pushed an irritable strand of greasy hair out of his eyes. "You think I'm stupid?" He shook the wrench in my face. "We both know you're holding out."

The wrench dangled in Frank's hand like a gaveling hook. It was a sure bet that it would be embedded in my head if I didn't find an escape hatch.

"We're gonna see if you're leveling with me Eddie," he said. "I guarantee we're gonna find out." Grabbing me by the shirt, he slammed me against the wall. His hand slid tighter around the wrench. "Tell me where the food is."

Crunch time had arrived. Frank would kill someone for giving him a sideway glance and then stop at a diner for eggs and coffee. If I wanted to survive, I'd need to move fast.

I looked from corner to corner. My rifle was propped against the rear wall of the room. I could try and grab it but Frank would be on me before I ever took a step.

"Don't let them piss on you out there," said the little guy in my head. *"Put your game hat on. The clock is ticking."*

"You asked for this cowboy." Frank's grainy expression baked with rage. He hoisted the pipe wrench in the air.

That was the golden moment. For a brief instant, the weapon suspended over his head and poised to strike, Frank stood there defenseless.

"Now!" screamed the voice in my head.

Without warning, I rammed my knee into Frank's groin. Groaning, he loosened the grip on the wrench but still wouldn't drop it.

Bolting across the cellar floor, I headed straight for the rifle. Frank shot an arm out and clipped me on the neck. I tripped and fell to the floor with a thud.

Glaring, his eyes black as polluted waters, there was no mistaking the impenetrable look of hatred that fogged Frank's eyes. "You're a dead man," he announced. Stinking of whiskey and born to kill, he raised the wrench into striking position again.

Frank moved in like a tiger gathering lunch. He swung the wrench but I rolled away, only inches from being struck. Lunging out across the room, I quickly grabbed the rifle, twisted around and jabbed it at his gut like a bayonet.

"Don't make a move!" I yelled.

Across the room, Beth cowered behind a rusted lawnmower.

Frank stopped cold. Uncertainty waved over his face as if he were considering the odds of getting hit by a bolt of lightning during a thunderstorm.

"You know what I think?" Frank grinned nervously. "I think you don't have the backbone to pull the trigger." He took a step closer.

I didn't know if I had backbone or not but couldn't allow Frank to see any trace of human frailty. If he sensed hesitation, he'd break my wings as if I were a wounded sparrow in the woods.

"I'm telling you, stay back and drop the wrench." I jammed the gun tighter in his stomach.

Still warnings didn't carry much weight, especially in the eyes of a hardened criminal bloated with hard liquor and moral degradation.

As a boy I once had a friend named Paul Heywood. The neighborhood kids called him Dynamite because he liked blowing things up. Sometimes he hooked a rifle out of his father's gun cabinet and sneaked into the woods to shoot tin cans up at Tracer's garbage dump.

"Go ahead." Dynamite shoved the rifle in my hands one day when he spotted a robin seated on the wire of a telephone pole. "Knock the feathers off it."

"No way." I pushed the weapon back in his hands.

"You're a pussy." He sniggered.

"Am not!" I shouted and walked away.

But I was. I didn't have what it takes to kill something.

After everything that happened over the last thirty days, I wondered if that primal instinct might have changed. I asked myself if I had the unrefined savagery to squeeze a trigger and put a chunk of metal in a man's heart. It occurred to me that I might never have the opportunity to answer that question. Furthermore I didn't even know if the gun's safety was on or off. Then again, that didn't matter either.

"You really think you got the stones to shoot me cowboy?" Frank took another dangerous step forward.

I was scared, petrified actually. But it wasn't Frank's unwavering glare that nailed me to a cross of dread. I had secrets, and right about now, I was keeping the biggest one of my life.

The gun had no bullets.

16

Missing Persons

Fear alone is an unreliable tool for survival. Sometimes it makes you run fast. Other times it bolts your feet to the floor, hampering a quick getaway. In my case, locked inside the walls of a twelve by twelve cellar, neither scenario panned out as a reliable means of escape.

I glanced at the gun, empty of bullets. If I squeezed the trigger, the only resulting impact would be me being beaten bloody by a madman.

Frank probed my every move. If I showed a hint of weakness, there'd be no hesitation. He'd stick a knife in my throat, bone deep. The guy would have made one hell of a good poster child for advocates in favor of capital punishment.

Back when the world was still online, I read about this young woman who got abducted by a guy named Charles Biggs. Along with his cronies, Biggs drove her to a secluded lake. He raped the girl, shot her in the head and then forced her under water until she drowned. After he was arrested, lawyers argued that Biggs had emotional difficulties, perhaps relating back to childhood that caused him to commit murder. What the hell was there to argue about? The guy was crazy. Now take him out behind a shed and shoot him.

Before the world fell to pieces, human rights activists protested the idea of capital punishment. They said it would cost twenty times more money to execute someone as opposed to keeping them in jail. I can't figure it out. How much is the price of a bullet? You do the math.

That might sound cruel but I can tell you this. If those same human rights activists were standing in my shoes and staring into the cold eyes of a killer, attitudes would change. Figuratively speaking, if we would have taken out the trash instead of letting it pile up in the streets, there would be no Frank and I wouldn't be wondering if I'd be alive in the next ten minutes.

"What's wrong?" Frank leaned coolly against a cellar post, his thumb hooked in his belt. "You gonna shoot me or not cowboy?" He tried to remain composed but I could see it in his expression. A hot bed of anger metastasized underneath his gruff exterior. If I gave him an opening, he'd cut me to confetti.

"Don't do anything stupid," I warned.

"You should give me that thing before you hurt yourself." His eyes, hard as nails, glanced at the gun. "We could work this out," he suggested. "But if we don't? Things will get ugly."

Staring at Frank, I tried to untangle the gravity of his threats. Other than a documentary I saw on television about John Wayne Gacy, I didn't know much about the criminal mind. The commentator said most killers were controlling and had a skewed sense of reality. Just those few words painted a portrait of Frank. To him, people weren't human beings; they were puppets for his amusement.

Standing across the cellar, Beth stared at the rifle as if it were a Medusa. Quiet desperation blanketed her face. Still I didn't understand her motives. Making allies with Frank made about as much sense as staging an armed robbery at Rockefeller Center for a two dollar hot dog.

"Last chance." Frank took another step closer. "Hand over the weapon and nobody gets hurt."

Standing there, I thought back to my boss at the car dealership. He used to kick back on a leather chair in his office, hands folded behind his head, and bark out insults.

"Are you stupid Slate?" he'd ask. "That's it, isn't it? You're stupid. If you want to survive in the car business, you need to be a good liar. That's your problem," he said. "You got the talent but don't know how to lie. Take a lesson from politicians. They do it all the time, got it?" He crumbled up a piece of paper and shot it in a waste basket.

Yeah, I got it alright, but I didn't like it. Talking a customer into buying a Corvette when all they needed was a used jalopy to run to the grocery store wasn't my specialty. Still I couldn't deny that lying was a prerequisite in my line of work, and staring into Frank's uncompromising eyes, I knew I'd need to draw on those skills and make the biggest sales pitch of my career. In fact, my life depended on it.

Frank inched forward.

"I'm not telling you again. Don't move." I raised the rifle, dead center on Frank's right eye.

"You think I give a rat's ass about a gun pointed at my head?" He grinned stiffly. A slight dribble of sweat dabbed the side of his neck. "Back in prison a gunshot is like a kiss on the cheek. You ever see a man get his head kicked with a boot until it falls apart like the peels on an orange?" He took another step. If he had a bottle of polish, he could have reached out and buffed the end of the gun barrel.

An eerie recognition of what life had become shined in Frank's black eyes. Even before the gas pumps went dry, the world had become desensitized. Be it greed, war, famine or empty gas tanks, people got numb. Instead of hitting baseballs down at Sam Miller's field, kids sat at home eradicating zombies on computer screens. That's what happened to Frank. Somewhere along the road, he shut off the spigot of empathy and not even the threat of a bullet could deter his drive for dominance and control.

"You gonna go psycho on me Frank?" I locked on his every move.

"What do you think?" He gave a wily grin.

We stared at each other, both refusing to give up our respective positions. But the standoff wouldn't last long. Something needed to be done. Trust me. When you're face to face with a killer and holding an empty rifle, you wouldn't believe how fast something needs to be done.

Gulping down fear, I shoved the barrel tight against Frank's stomach. For a minute his unremarkable grin faded.

"You think I won't shoot?" My expression remained cold: a block of ice.

Shadows of uncertainty crossed Frank's dark eyes. After a long pause he took a slow step backward.

"That a boy." I motioned towards the corner of the cellar. "Now sit down. Keep your hands where I can see them."

"I get it cowboy," said Frank. "This is your fifteen minutes of fame. Enjoy it. It won't last." He hesitantly lowered himself against the rear wall of the room.

I left out a silent sigh of relief. It was quite a performance, the sales pitch of the century. I should have been nominated for an Emmy.

At the same time I wasn't stupid. Frank wouldn't be subdued long. I could see him studying me, already making contingency plans for a hostile takeover.

"What now? Are we gonna hold hands and sing campfire songs?" Frank draped an arm over his knee.

"Be quiet." I tried to sound tough. That's never been my style. I'm that guy who clips supermarket coupons from the newspaper and has a takeout menu from Wong's Chinese Palace stuck to the refrigerator with a magnet.

One thing I did know. Frank was patient as a terrorist. He'd wait. He'd wait as long as it took, and when I made a mistake? He'd launch an attack.

I glanced down at the rifle in my hands and tried not to look conspicuous.

Am I a moron?

Yup, the jury was unanimous. I'm a goddamn moron.

Last year I bought the rifle and a box of ammo for home defense. Later that summer I took a Caribbean cruise onboard a luxury liner called The Lovebird. With swimming pools, barbecue pits and exotic nightclubs, it probably now floated aimless in the middle of the Atlantic.

One night I found a red fedora blowing around the deck outside of Shaky Jake's Rumba Lounge. Man, I probably looked like a first class geek walking around poolside wearing that thing. When I returned home from the cruise, I tossed the fedora on top of the box of ammo that had been stuffed in an upstairs closet. I admit it; I'm a pack rat. Broken egg beaters, old VHS tapes, even a foot massager. You couldn't open the door without getting clubbed in the head with an ironing board. With all the junk, I never did find what happened to the ammunition or even the that stupid red fedora that I found during vacation. At the time it didn't matter much, but looking at the Remington cribbed in my arms? Right about now it was the only thought in my mind.

Glancing over at Beth, I still couldn't reconcile the idea of her teaming up with Frank. He was the classic portrait of a woman abuser who regarded females as property. From Frank's vantage point, Beth was spoils of war, bought and paid for.

"Tell me the truth. What are you doing with him?" I asked Beth.

"Don't tell him anything." Frank shot her a stern look of warning. Beth lowered her eyes.

"Nobody asked you to speak," I warned him.

"Tell me something." Frank wobbled his knee from side to side. "Did you ever make love to her?"

"I said shut up." I jammed the barrel of the gun underneath Frank's chin. I'm not sure what I was thinking in that desperate moment, but even with no bullets, I almost pulled the trigger.

Frank's arm remained draped over his knee. He looked confident and self-assured; a spider preparing an evening meal. I had to stay focused. If I faltered, I'd be caught in the web.

"You must have confidence in that woman." Frank smirked. "The old saying is true. Love is blind. If you think she's so trustworthy, hand her the gun," he dared me. "Go ahead. Give it to her."

Beth finally looked up from the floor. "You don't understand Eddie. You can trust me." She stepped forward.

"Don't move Beth."

"Eddie..."

"I said don't move." I kept the rifle pointed out in front of me.

My thoughts were tangled up wire. I didn't know what to believe any longer.

Before the world shattered, sometimes I sat outside on my deck on summer evenings. You know, drink a cold one and breathe in the stars. The teenage years must have been a happy time because I reminisce about them a lot. Back then the world still didn't beat the hell out of me with taxes, company cutbacks and faithless romances. It was okay to live in a shoebox and not be able to afford a hamburger at a fast food joint. All that mattered was falling in love.

I met Beth at a dance in high school. I was a wallflower and would never be captain of the football team, but she still liked me. Even more, I was crazy about her. Whenever she smiled, I swear the sun rose over the ocean.

Standing in a cellar holding a rifle, again I looked in the eyes of a girl I once held so close that I could feel her heart beat against my chest. That was long ago. Setting aside those magic moments, I looked at her now and had to ask myself this one question; after all these years; how well did I really know her?

"Hey cowboy, you feeling alright?" asked Frank. "It seemed like you were drifting there for a minute. I wouldn't get too comfortable. I sure as hell won't." His rigid fingers dug in the dirt floor of the cellar.

"I warned you, shut up."

Regardless of the tough talk, I don't like confrontation. My idea of getting physical is ten pushups with an open bag of potato chips on the coffee table. Still I changed over the last weeks. Put a man in a ghetto and either he'll learn how to survive in the elements and eat from a garbage can or die from cold and starvation.

"Still trying to play the hero?" Frank taunted. "Pull the trigger."

"I said shut up!" I raised the Remington.

"Eddie, stop!" Beth's voice rang out from a corner of the room. Her face was an open grate of panic. "Put the gun down."

"What?" I tilted my head in confusion.

"You have to trust me," she said in a soft voice. "You've got to stop. Give me the weapon."

"Are you insane?"

"I won't let you shoot him." She stepped forward, directly in front of Frank.

"Move away Beth."

My mind whirled, a jet plane spinning out of control. Beth's devotion to Frank didn't add up. People blindly followed madmen like Manson or David Koresh because they knew how to manipulate the weak and gullible. She didn't fit that bill. Still there she stood, defending the guilty.

"Stop now Eddie. Please stop." Beth raised her hands.

"I said move out of the way."

"Don't listen to him," Frank ordered her. "If he kills me, you'll regret it the rest of your life."

Beth's lips trembled, a volcano ready to erupt. She held firm to a protective stance in front of Frank. "If you want to kill him, you'll have to shoot me first," she insisted.

"Have you lost your mind?" I asked. "Beth, what's wrong with you? He's dangerous!"

"Please Eddie, you can't kill him."

"Why?"

"Please don't..."

"I said why?" I shouted loudly.

Beth pursed her lips in a cross between fear and rage. Finally she screamed, "Because he has my daughter!"

17

Something in the Night

Beth stared at me, riddled in fear.

"You told me your daughter went to your sister's house."

"I lied," she said.

Seated Indian-style on the dirt floor, Frank shook his head. "See what I mean? She led you into a trap. We were gonna steal your supplies. Now that she's caught, she's telling lies about her daughter. Women," he said. "Never trust them."

My head tilted towards Beth. Even in a compromised moment, her blue eyes appeared young and guiltless. "Is that true?"

"A twisted truth," she said and shifted a step away from Frank. "When the oil stopped, everyone went crazy. I thought we'd be okay, at least until help arrived. But the days passed and nobody came. Then the power went out. It got cold. People were fighting in the streets. I heard gunshots at night. My daughter Ashley was terrified. We were going to Rockport where my sister lives, but with no fuel, travel wasn't only impossible, it was dangerous."

I shifted my gaze to Frank and then back to Beth. "How does he figure into this?"

"I didn't sleep for days," Beth said fearfully. "Bundling up blankets, we went down in the basement where it was warmer. Finally I passed out from exhaustion. When I woke up, Ashley was missing." She wiped a tear from her cheek. "I went upstairs to look for her and found Frank in the front room. He told me that unless I did exactly as he said, I'd never see my daughter again."

Frank laughed. "Are you really gonna buy this performance? Give her the gun and she'd mow us both down."

My head reeled in all directions. I didn't know what to believe. Frank would steal his mother's shoes and then sell them for cigarettes. Given the chance, he'd cut my throat.

Looking at Beth, she might have been telling the truth about her daughter. Still she joined forces with Frank. That didn't only make her a suspect; that made her potentially lethal.

A loud bang upstairs derailed my train of thought.

Frank's eyes swung to the top of the staircase. "It sounds like we got company. The more the merrier."

"Quiet," I whispered.

"What's wrong?" asked Frank. "You got the rifle. Put it to good use."

"I said quiet." My heart wrapped like a hammer as I peered up the flight of stairs.

"You're in deep," the voice in my head said. *"Stay alert. Remember, you don't have any bullets. In layman's terms, you're screwed. If you get sloppy, the only shots fired will be from an intruder's gun."*

A runner of sweat dribbled down my cheek. I felt no more stable than the San Andres fault. It was just a matter of time, perhaps moments, before everything cracked wide open. "Maybe it's just the wind."

"Sure it is." A grin played over Frank's lips. "And I'm the pope."

Listening close, patterns of footsteps inched across the floor and stopped near the top of the stairs.

"Don't take your eyes off the ball," said the little voice in my head. *"If you do, the game is over."*

That was easier said than done. An intruder walked around upstairs, a killer sat in the corner of the cellar waiting for me to make a mistake, and a woman I once loved stared at me with unsettled eyes.

"Are you listening?" the little voice spoke up again. *"There's probably no way out of this outside of killing someone. Stay alert. Concentrate. I'm not sure you have what it takes."*

That was the problem; I didn't have what it takes.

Don't get me wrong. I was a smart kid. I could have been a doctor or a lawyer. Instead I sold automobiles on a car lot. At the time I figured it was just a hell of a lot easier than performing open heart surgery.

Frank didn't have my grades in school but his education flourished behind prison walls. He had street smarts. While he served hard time at the state pen, my familiarity of the law didn't extend beyond an unpaid parking ticket. Mingling with killers or watching someone take a knife to the throat was second nature to him. Given both the chance and manners learned in prison, he'd take me down, fast and furious.

That's where the trouble reared its ugly head. I wasn't focused, and for not more than a measly second, I took my eye off the ball and turned my attention to the noise at the top of the staircase.

Fierce as a lion, Frank rocketed off the floor. Before I had a chance to raise the gun, his fingers slid around my throat.

"Drop the weapon." He squeezed hard.

I struggled to break free but swapping fists had never been my strong point. I also wasn't a health fanatic who spooned health muck for breakfast and popped steroids. Frank, on the other hand, spent his years lifting weights behind bars and surviving a hostile environment. In a fight, he had the primal edge.

In a desperate attempt to break his stronghold, I rammed a knee into Frank's gut. He buckled but wouldn't break. Frank returned the favor by ripping a stiff fist to my ribs. Gasping for air, the gun flew out of my hands and on the floor. Accenting his point, he knuckled me in the jaw. The taste of blood painted my tongue and lips.

Fast and deliberate, Frank lunged across the room and picked up the pipe wrench that was on the floor. He banged it slowly in his hand. "It's closing time cowboy. It's time to shut her down and lock things up." Springing forward, he headed straight at me. Except that a loud noise erupted from the top of the stairs, he might have finished me off right there.

Frank stopped cold and stared up the steps. "Whoever you are, you're next!"

The only answer came in the form of something inaudible, threatening, and not quite human.

18

Shadow's Land

An animal's sensory world is different than a human. Dogs rely more on noses and ears than sight. They also don't exist in the past or future; they live for the moment, assessing how comfortable they are chewing on a bone or sprawled out on the porch on a lazy summer afternoon. Mostly they enjoy different scents and sounds. Other times they detest them. Dogs also know when people like them. Likewise, they can sense a threat.

When Jimmy Stokes met his fate by way of a bullet to the head, his dog Shadow adopted me as the new master. Beaten down and about to become one of Frank's casualties, I could only imagine what the animal might have thought when he heard hostile noises rising from inside the house.

Shadow couldn't talk and didn't know much in terms of human language. Still he understood the look in his master's eyes at dinnertime, and when the leash came out, he knew it was time to go for a walk. He loved walking. The smell of grass and all the scents in the air made him happy.

But something happened while he sat in his house with the master. There was a loud bang and the master fell to the floor. Nuzzling a cold nose against him, there was no movement, no jiggling of keys to go and take a ride in the car. Shadow didn't comprehend death but he understood loss. Resting his head against the master's chest, he didn't feel the thump of a heartbeat. Something changed. Suddenly, all that he loved was gone.

When the master fell down and stopped moving, Shadow remembered the scent of a man, a very bad man. The stale odor of his sweat clung in the dog's nostrils. He wouldn't forget that smell. Instinct urged him to attack the bad man, but still he wouldn't leave the master's side, not even for the sake of vengeance.

Soon the bad man went away and Shadow was alone again.

No, not alone. Someone else was downstairs in the basement, only this man was different. Unlike the other one, this man had a good smell.

"Come here boy." The good man in the basement whistled.

Shadow's ear perked up. He even wagged his tail. Still, a soldier on the battlefield, he wouldn't abandon his post. The dog rested its head on the master's chest.

Not long after, the good man in the basement left and everything grew quiet again. This time he truly was alone.

Totally alone.

Getting up, three times Shadow lumbered towards a door that stood ajar, and three times he turned around and went back to where the master had fallen. Nudging his nose against his owner's neck, there was still no movement. Finally Shadow turned, pushed the door open with his nose and plodded out into the darkness.

Scanning the trees and empty roads with black and white vision, Shadow grew frightened. He had never been all alone on the streets. Cruel people were abroad. He sensed danger.

Sniffing again, for an instant he caught a whiff of a familiar scent and his ears perked up. It was the smell of the good man, the one in the basement of his house. Just up ahead, he trudged along the road.

Shadow's paws ached from where he stepped in an icy puddle of water but still he hurried towards him.

"Hey," the man said in surprise as he turned around. "Come on over boy."

Shadow held his distance for a minute. Finally he made a shy approach. Reaching out slowly, the man scratched him behind the ears, just the way the master used to do. It made him feel good. It made him feel safe.

"Come on Shadow," the man said and began to walk.

Shadow knew this man would be his friend, his owner, his new master. The dog would follow him, count on him. Protect him.

Shadow knew little about the new master. Still he sensed something in the man's demeanor as he approached a house near the end of an alley. The man stiffened. A slight scent of sweat balled up on his skin. Something was wrong.

"Okay Shadow." The man bent down and patted the dog on the head. "Stay here, know what I mean?"

Shadow did know. He didn't comprehend much human gibberish, but did understand when someone told him to stay.

Lowering himself on the ground, the dog sneezed and tilted his head curiously as the man crawled through a window near the bottom of the house and disappeared.

Shadow wasn't cold but still the icy weather made him tingle. He looked from side to side at the darkened landscape. A sense of abandonment crushed in on him. He missed the master, both the old and the new. He was also hungry. Licking his chops, Shadow left out a slight whine.

Sniffing, the dog suddenly stopped cold. Something bad, the kind of smell that made the hair bristle on the back of his spine, breezed in the wind. He immediately recognized the scent. It was the same stench that he smelled when the bad man, the one who hurt his master, was in the house. That smell made him feel angry. Protective.

Violent.

Shadow eyed an open door that banged against the house in the cold wind. Getting up, he plodded over to it and slipped in the doorway.

Once inside the house, the smell grew stronger. It filtered up from a flight of steps. Moving forward, the dog's tail knocked over a lamp on a table that made a loud racket when it banged off the floor. Shadow jumped at the noise but didn't waver. The bad man's stink, as did the animal's rage, grew stronger as he approached the cellar doorway. Somewhere in the bowels of the house, an enemy was abroad.

Shadow's limbs stiffened. Crouching, the dog expelled a low but threatening growl as he readied for battle.

19

Hostile Takeovers

Something moved at the top of the steps. Maybe it was just a poacher getting out of the wind. Then again, maniacs ran rampant as rats in walls.

"We got company." Staring at the steps, Frank's eyes were targeted as hollow point bullets. He grabbed me by the scruff of the neck and held the pipe wrench firmly in his hand. "You hear me up there asshole?" he shouted. "Show yourself. If you try anything stupid, I'll twist this guy's head off." His fingers dug into the back of my neck.

A white moon shined in a window at the top of the steps and expelled muddy light. Something stirred. A dark figure held low to the ground and moved from one side of the doorway to the next.

Frank's face twisted in uncertainty. "You hear me?" he said again. "If you don't show yourself I'll..."

A ferocious growl sounded out in the quiet confines of the house. In a sudden frenzy, Shadow barreled down the steps. The dog's jaws snapped with intent on eradicating every impulse of his adversary.

Frank swung the wrench. Too late. Shadow leapt and bowled him over. The wrench flew from Frank's hand, clanged on the floor and landed in the far corner of the cellar. Warding off a frontal attack, Frank grabbed the dog and pushed him away. Shadow's fierce jaws bore down and clamped on to Frank's shoulder. Like a stubborn lumberjack trying to remove a difficult stump, the dog's head whipped from side to side.

I stood there immobilized. Part of me wanted to run. With the dog occupying Frank, I saw a window of escape.

Turning to look at Beth, her anxious face twisted in fear.

"Get him off!" Frank tried to peel the animal away. "Get him off or you'll never see your daughter again!"

"Please." Beth grabbed my arm. A river of fear flooded down her cheeks.

The dog had become the first line of defense and a deterrent against any retaliatory strikes imposed by Frank. Still if I didn't do something, a young girl like Beth's daughter all alone on the streets? With little food and water available, prospects for survival were grim.

"Shadow!" I shouted in a commanding tone, not expecting the dog to retreat.

However, Shadow grudgingly unhinged his jaws. The animal backed away, never removing its tight stare from the immediate threat.

"Get that mutt out of here." Frank fingered a rinse of blood on his shoulder.

"No chance." I patted Shadow on the head. "Don't make any sudden moves and there won't be trouble."

"You really think you're in control of the situation?" Frank turned apple red with anger. "Loose the dog or Beth's brat daughter dies. Is that clear enough?"

"Please Eddie." Worry and tears bellied up under Beth's eyes. "He has Ashley. If we don't do as he says, I'll never find her."

Looking at the terrified expression playing over Beth's face, finally I picked up the gun and turned it towards Frank.

"Shadow." I whistled at the dog and glanced up the stairs. "Go on."

Growling and sneezing, the dog reluctantly climbed the steps and disappeared. Jimmy Stokes taught his pooch well.

"Satisfied Frank?" I put the gun barrel tight against his cheekbone. "Now where's the girl?"

While a dog with teeth the size of tree trimmers disturbed him, Frank didn't share the same sense of urgency with a gun pointed at his head. Prison life toughened him up. He got used to killers and thieves. My guess was that a half starved car salesman who drank light beer and watched reruns of Seinfeld while dipping into a bag of potato chips didn't qualify as a viable menace.

None of it really mattered in the end. After all, there were no bullets in the gun. If I pulled the trigger, there'd be an empty click. Frank would vault off the floor with fists balled into sledgehammers. The game would be over.

"Beth?" She turned towards me. I glanced at a rusted toolbox on a shelf. "There's rope in there. Get it."

Hesitating, Beth walked over to the box and opened it. Reaching in, she pulled out a raveled up white wash line that I stuck in there God knows when.

I turned to Frank. "Back up against that pole. Move slow. No tricks."

Crossing his arms defiantly, Frank smirked. He was determined to show his superiority by way of noncompliance.

I'm not lucky, did I mention that? I couldn't get ahead on money if someone offered me a twenty spot for a ten dollar roll of quarters. I didn't know how to bluff. That's a detriment when it came to being a car salesman and probably the reason my boss viewed me as a failure. I simply didn't lie good. That couldn't be the case today. I had to carry out the ultimate sham. Frank needed to believe I'd shoot him, even as the bullets lay buried in the upstairs closet under a dented up red fedora.

"Last chance Frank," My finger jostled the trigger. "You wanna die? Give me a reason to fire."

A thin line of doubt crystallized in Frank's expression. After a minute he finally backed up against the support beam in the corner of the room.

"Tie his hands," I told Beth. "Make it tight."

Stepping to the rear of the beam, Beth cautiously knotted Frank's hands securely around the pole. I lowered my weapon, just a bit.

"So cowboy, it appears we got ourselves a situation." Frank's chiseled face, muddied with grime, flickered in candlelight as his thin lips curled. "What's the next move?" he asked. "Do we wait for the army to roll in on snowmobiles and read me my rights?"

"You got no rights Frank." I stared him down. "Now answer. Where's Beth's daughter?"

"You must think I'm an idiot," he said. "The kid is leverage. You want her back?" he asked. "Maybe we can make a deal."

"What deal?" I eyed him carefully.

"Untie me first. Let me go and I'll tell you where she is."

"You're lying."

"Maybe, maybe not." Frank shifted against the pole, struggling to loosen his restraints. "Looks like you'll just have to trust me on that one."

"Trust you?" I laughed. "Forget it."

"Then I guess it's gonna be a long night cowboy." He stared with disdain.

Pinching the fleshy part of her hand, Beth looked on from the corner of the room.

If I had bullets, I might have shot one of Frank's kneecaps to give him some incentive to cooperate, but I didn't have much nerve and even less ammo. Waiting for him to get hungry or thirsty enough to talk also wasn't an option. Beth's daughter was alone out there in the jungle. Time pressed in like a vice.

"It's simple. If you want to see the kid alive again, let me go." Frank hung tough. "That's the terms."

I glared at him, wondering what to do next. His smug expression hung over the room like a stink bomb.

"What are you waiting for?" Frank dared me and glanced at the gun. "The game is getting old partner. If you want me dead, pull the trigger, but you won't pull it, will you?" he said smugly. "For all I know, you were one of those shitty human rights activists protesting the death penalty down in Washington on Saturday afternoons. Guys like you aren't built for murder."

Some of that was true. I'd avoid a fight at all costs, let alone sinking a bullet into someone's skull. Then again. I went from eating steak dinners and HD television to living in a cellar and scraping cold beans out of a tin can, all inside a month. Regression had become a way of life.

"You should get real with yourself." Frank laughed and spit on the floor. "What are you gonna do, drive me to Gitmo and interrogate me? You're not the Gestapo. Like I said, you got no guts for murder."

Standing there staring at Frank, I wasn't convinced as to whether I had guts or not. Certainly I had no bullets. However, looking down at the floor, I was sure of one thing.

I had a big pipe wrench.

20

Matters of Trust

"Anyone got a cigarette?" Frank kicked at the floor with his boot. He continually twisted his wrists and tried to free himself from his fetters.

Ignoring him, I turned in Beth's direction. Her face sunk in a moat of fear.

Standing there, I couldn't help but to retreat into the past, long before the oil crisis emerged. Looking back, time passed quickly. If you're a teenager still green around the ears, you probably think that people turning thirty are fossilized and should be put on display at the Smithsonian. Don't blink; you'll get there soon enough.

Back then, Beth and I parked by the lake on warm starry nights, listening to our favorite songs on the radio. But those romantic teenage memories were only echoes of a former world. They had since been replaced with a killer's frigid stare.

"I don't want any trouble," said Frank, tapping his foot. "I know," he conceded. "I went a little crazy, right? People do that in a catastrophe. With what's going on, half the country is delusional. Even a shitty little car salesman like yourself isn't safe to follow the law. Push someone far enough and they'll fall off a cliff. That's what I did," he said. "I tumbled off the cliff.

Given the right circumstances, even you might kill someone. Everyone wants to be self-righteous, but in the end? You're just like me."

"I'll never be like you Frank," I corrected.

"Is that right?" He answered smartly. "Look who's pointing the gun."

Regardless of his antagonism, Frank's words carried some weight. Keep someone's head submerged in a cesspool long enough and eventually they'll suck the water into their lungs. Just a few weeks ago I couldn't have imagined surviving any of this. If I ran out of a tube of toothpaste it was a tragedy, but now? Instead of waiting for the noon lunch whistle over at the dealership, I'm toting around a rifle and getting ready, if need be, to end someone's life.

"I think you should go with the odds and let me go cowboy." Frank remained calm and unwavering. "It's your best chance."

"Best chance for what Frank?"

"To stay alive of course," he answered. "I'm not the forgiving type. I got a long memory. When I finally get loose, I'll kill you Eddie, you know that don't you? I'll kill you and spit on your grave. Beth and her daughter won't be far behind. You really want something like that on your conscience?"

I stared at Frank. Regardless of the cutting comments, I refused to turn away or show any signs of weakness.

"Tell me where the girl is Frank."

"First untie me," he bargained. "It's a matter of trust."

Trust was something good, reliable, and honest. Looking at Frank, all of those virtues were a waterless desert, swept away in the sands.

"Where is she Frank? I won't ask again."

"I'm telling you forget it," he said smartly.

I peered up the staircase. "You want me to bring the dog back? He's a playful little pup, isn't he?"

A nervous edge cemented in the corners of Frank's eyes but still he remained calm. "A dog like that could rip my throat out in a heartbeat," he said. "You'd like that. Then again you'd never find out where the kid is. What's her name, Ashley?" He winked at Beth and then his face turned back to stone. "Get it straight. If I die, the brat goes with me."

Frank was stalling but also hinted at the truth. Jimmy Stokes' German Sheppard, big as a house, was well versed in the art of combat. If the animal attacked again and couldn't be contained, he'd kill Frank. Ashley might be lost forever.

"Please." Beth folded her hands. "Just tell me where my daughter is. I promise nobody will hurt you."

Frank studied her pain. After a minute he said, "I can see you're afraid. You should be. Most of the jails were unlocked when the oil disaster hit. It isn't just killers out there. Pedophiles are roaming the streets. I'd hate like hell to have an eight year old daughter alone in the wild."

For an instant I swore Beth's hair nearly lifted off the nape of her neck. She stood there frozen in fear, elbows pressed stiffly into her sides.

"Shut your mouth Frank," I warned.

"I shared a cellblock with a guy named Jason Hens," he forged ahead. "That guy sodomized more pre-teens than there are chickens in a poultry farm. Once he even hogtied a little girl, drove her to Shasta Lake and then strangled her with a coat hanger. Afterwards he stuffed the remains in a garbage bag, put some rocks inside for weight, and then tossed her in the lake. The cops fished her body out of the water a week later. Nothing left of course but dental records." Frank grinned hideously. "Is that the kind of thing you're worried about?"

"I said shut up!" I yelled.

Turning my head towards Beth, her hands trembled. She glared at Frank with a fevered look of bottomless hatred. Suddenly she let out a loathsome scream and lunged forward.

Pulling back her arm, she throttled Frank with a closed fist to the side of his face. The blow was enough to make his head whip to one side.

"You took my baby!" she screamed. Finally she turned to me and grabbed me by the shoulders. "Please Eddie, we need to get it out of him. He knows where Ashley is. He knows!" Her face shattered and fell to pieces.

I never had kids. Most of my friends got married and made babies after college. I continued on with the single life. While they changed diapers, I cruised the Jersey shore in a beat up Chevy with the radio blaring. At sunrise I stood on the beach in the Wildwoods and listened as waves crashed against the ocean reef. I was young. Irresponsible. Life was good. But on the day the oil disaster arrived, everything cracked, and as I peered into Beth's desperate eyes, the stricken expression of a mother's anguish, it broke altogether.

Beth dragged her trembling fingers down her cheeks and rocked in place on the floor. Her pained stare pleaded, not with words, but eyes that begged for mercy. Finally she sunk to the ground on weak knees. Retreating into a fetal position, she began to sob.

"That's right darlin'," Frank mocked. "You should cry. I took the brat, and if you want to see her alive again? I'd think about untying me real fast." He turned his head and spit blood from where Beth broke open his lip. "You'll have to do one hell of a lot better than a slap to the jaw if you want to get any information out of me. Hey cowboy?" He turned to me and sneered. "You ready to cooperate and finish things?"

Taking a deep breath, I leaned the gun against the wall and picked up the pipe wrench that lay on the floor.

"I'm ready," I concurred.

21

Lines you don't Cross

"Where's the girl Frank?" I tapped the pipe wrench in my hand.

"There's a new martial in town, eh?" Frank's wrists twisted in the ropes. He tried to remain composed but uncertainty crystallized over his clammy skin.

During Germany's occupation of Western Europe, atrocities ran rampant in the concentration camps. People's hands were put in boiling water until the skin under their fingernails came off like gloves. Cutting or twisting off ears was also a favorite technique among many of fiendish devices too horrible to depict. In short, the Nazis got medieval on their victims. Standing there holding a wrench that a few weeks ago had been used for nothing more than to fix the plumbing on the toilet, it struck me as to how brutal the world had become.

"Tell me where the girl is." I turned the wrench in my hand.

Sweat beaded up on Frank's forehead. His hands squirmed in the restraints. Doubt, a hurricane about to make landfall with no definitive point of contact, played over his damp expression. His shoulders grew tense as he stared at the wrench.

"Take it easy cowboy." Frank's raspy breath sounded out in the stagnant air. "You really think you got what it takes to use that thing?"

"Stop stalling," I warned. "Tell me where Ashley is."

"You're looking at me like I'm a terrorist," he said, a slight shake in his voice. "I was a soldier, did I mention that? I worked on the demolition squad. Who the hell would ever think they'd let a guy like me blow things up. I fought in the Gulf for assholes like you." His eyes rolled up in contempt. "When I got out of the army, I didn't look for trouble. Saturday nights I'd go down to the local bar and tie one on, maybe find some local talent, take them back to my apartment and screw the balls off them. The good old days, right?"

"What's your point?" I asked impatiently.

"I got issues," he said. "None of this is my fault."

"It's always someone else's fault, isn't it Frank?" I glared at him but couldn't help wondering why someone didn't sprinkle rat poison in his cereal a long time ago. Nope. People were too busy tuning into talk shows and misinformed shrinks insistent on coddling the bad element because their daddy's gave them a slap back in puberty.

Again Frank glanced at the wrench, then back to me, then back to the wrench again. He tried to determine if I had the stomach for torturing someone. In that tense moment, I tried to do the same.

"There isn't much more to talk about." Fidgeting, he eyed the exit stairs between facial tics. "It looks like you'll have to drop the hammer."

"Don't tempt me."

Frank tilted his head and considered my sincerity. His untiring glare could have burned a hole in my head faster than a cigarette against a cotton shirt. "You don't get it, do you?"

"Get what?" I tilted my head.

"Killers aren't trusted," Frank said. "They're feared. That's what keeps their victims in check: fear of retribution. There are lines you don't cross with a killer. If you do, payment gets expensive and you could end up with a switchblade in the heart. That's what killers do, but you?" Frank grinned doubtfully. "You're no killer. You're a car salesman Eddie. You want me to be afraid of that?"

A noise upstairs shifted my attention and made me fidget but it was nothing more than a rat scurrying through plaster walls.

"You see what I mean? You fall apart if a pin drops." Frank mocked. "You still think the military or some other unsung hero is going to roll into town and save your ass. Forget it," he said. "The boys in uniform are busy squelching riots in the cities. Places like Philadelphia and New York are disaster zones. In case you haven't figured it out yet, we're all alone out here."

The thought scared me, maybe because an air of truth breathed in the words. Help, at best, was probably still weeks away. When the disaster struck, transportation and modern convenience fell like dominos. Not even the farmers could get fuel for tractors to produce crops. Food would be impossible to find. The upper class population, the elite two percent of America that drove around in sunglasses and expensive Mercedes would now be reduced to growing backyard bean gardens and guarding tomato plants with a wooden club.

"Do you smell that?" Frank sniffed. "It's the scent of dread," he said. "Admit it. You won't fire the gun." He momentarily shifted his attention to the wrench and then back to me. "Remember what I said Eddie? There are lines you don't cross with a killer," he repeated. "Untie my wrists. If you do, I'll let you live."

Even shackled to a support beam in a grungy cellar, Frank tried to assume a position of authority and control. He just didn't believe that I'd hurt him.

I guess he had reasons for that. The idea of busting someone's nose with a fist scared the hell out of me. As a kid I sometimes got knocked around by bullies. I was the odd man out. It wasn't just the threat of getting beaten up. What if I really hurt someone during a fight? Even worse, what if I didn't hurt them enough and they got angry? They'd exact justice on me, that's what. In short, they'd pound me into eternity. I was a quiet guy who hated any kind of drama.

Well guess what? The drama had arrived, alive and in Technicolor.

"Where's the girl Frank?"

"Aren't you getting the message?" He laughed. "The only way you'll get information out of me is..."

I swung the pipe wrench, crashing it just above Frank's left kneecap. Frank left out a seeping groan but refused to howl out in pain.

"Tell me where Ashley is!" My face, apple red, glared as I shook the wrench.

Frank stared at me with an open mouth. Hints of a scornful grin were now deflated and confusion hung in his eyes like an irritable hair. He didn't believe I'd hit him or anticipate a reaction to his defiance. I'm not sure I did either.

Beth stayed in the corner of the room. However, something changed in her expression. Her trembling chin, only moments ago driven with sadness and horror for her missing daughter, now turned into a hard look of disdain. Her lips, once subtle and full, pulled back so far that her teeth were bared in contempt.

"I'm not gonna keep playing the game," I told Frank. "Where's the girl?"

"You gonna beat it out of me?" He glared, the blackness of death riding in his eyes.

"Tell me where she is."

"No chance."

"Answer me!" I shouted and rammed the wrench down on a wheelbarrow next to his head. Frank flinched. He looked scared. Damn scared. Still he wouldn't give up the secret.

"You think I'm afraid to die?" That smirk again, rebellious and daring. "You're gonna have to do better cowboy, comprende?" he said. "You're either gonna have to untie my wrists or kill me."

I stared at him, the wrench trembling in my hand.

Frank issued an ultimatum, kill him or set him free. Reasoning with him was futile. Brute force had been the only true dictator to control a guy like him and even that was failing. I stood there frozen, not knowing what to do next. That's the problem with guys like me. I lived the simple life. Eating pizza and drinking a beer at the pub while cheering on my favorite football team on TV spoiled me. I led a drama free life of leisure and didn't know how to resort to criminal behavior.

On the other hand, Beth did.

Beth's expression contorted into all angles of rage. Much like a lion protecting her young, the animal had got loose from the cage. Getting off the ground, she picked up the gun and barreled forward towards Frank uttering a scream and a war cry.

Frank drew back against the cellar's support beam. Unlike the air of hesitant indecision that hung over me, there was no mistaking the height of aggression in Beth's white knuckled fists.

"You took my baby!" She jabbed a finger in Frank's face. Lifting her shoe, she kicked Frank in the mid section.

Frank grunted, even buckled. Recovering quickly, he straightened himself up. "You want the kid?"

"Give her back!" Beth trembled with rage.

Frank's eyes narrowed down to slits. He leaned forward and looked her squarely in the eyes. "She'll be back in a wooden crate, six feet in the dirt."

Wet fury flooded down Beth's cheeks. Turning, she picked up the gun and shoved the barrel underneath Frank's chin. In that tense moment, remembrances of that sweet teenage girl I knew so many years ago disappeared. There was no mercy, no thought of consequence or moral action in her face. There was only uninhibited aggression and a mother's love for her missing child.

Beth let loose a bone chilling scream. Her finger squeezed at the gun's trigger, determined to open Frank's skull with a bullet.

"The church!" Frank pulled back and blurted out.

I grabbed Beth's arm and pushed the gun away.

"What?" I asked.

Frank breathed heavy. "She's at the church."

Pulling Beth aside in the upstairs of the house and out of Frank's earshot, I whispered, "You can't use the gun."

"What do you mean?" She tilted her head.

"Trust me," I said. "Don't fire it." I hesitated. "The rifle. It's empty. No bullets."

Fear rose in Beth's eyes. "What if Frank finds out?"

"He won't." I touched her arm assuredly.

But even though Frank's hands were tied, I wasn't taking any chances. I ran upstairs and dug through the closet where the ammo had last been seen. I found blankets, old VHS tapes, even that stupid red fedora that I picked up while on a cruise to the Bahamas. Still I couldn't find any bullets. Flinging the fedora on the floor, I hurried back down to the cellar.

Frank eyed me suspiciously. "You lose something cowboy?"

I glanced at Beth. She returned a worried look.

"Stay quiet," I told him, pointing the weapon.

Frank tied to a wooden post by a piece of rope wasn't the best insurance policy. Learned in the art of savagery, if he got loose and discovered that the rifle was empty, he'd kill me inside of a minute.

Keeping the gun on him, I cautiously walked over, bent down and took the radio out of Frank's pocket.

"Here." I handed it to Beth. "Keep this close. Stay connected. I'll go to the church. If your daughter is there, I'll find her.

"I should come with you," said Beth.

That wasn't the best plan. According to Frank, he locked Ashley in a room across town at Saint Jude's church. If I was exhausted, Beth looked shattered. She'd slow me up. Besides, Frank couldn't be left unattended. If he got loose, he'd come after us and wouldn't rest until we were dead.

"I'm scared Eddie." Beth touched my hand. It was soft. Warm.

"I'll find her," I said, but deep down, doubt swam in my mind.

A slight growl from upstairs alerted me to the idea that Shadow was still pacing the floors. "Listen," I said. "The dog is upstairs." I set the rifle down and glanced at the pipe wrench. "Keep that close. If anything happens, don't be afraid to use it."

Beth looked at me with a broken stare. "But if he's lying Eddie." A tear escaped from underneath her eye. "What if he's lying?"

I turned and looked at Frank. "If he's lying, then I'll kill him."

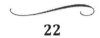

22

Search Parties

Icy wind punched me in the face when I walked outside. Scanning the darkened streets, the world looked secretive and treacherous. I had no idea if Frank told the truth about Ashley or if she was even alive.

Saint Jude's church was just across town, about a thirty minute walk.

Limping along on a bad leg, I turned down Center Avenue, passed Mount Pisgah Hotel, a once popular watering hole for the locals. Further down the street, a couple of vagrants passed around a half spent bottle of whiskey. They had a fire burning in a trash barrel and rubbed their hands together briskly to ward off the cold.

Crouching behind a pickup truck, I hurried quietly away, careful not to let them see me.

Little else moved in the streets. I did notice a woman peeking out from behind closed drapes, too frightened to come outside. The weight of her invisible stare, heavy as a cement slab, pressed down on my shoulders.

After awhile I reached a bridge leading to the west side of town. I pulled my radio out and hit the talk button.

"Beth?"

Static filled the radio. I held my breath.

"Eddie, is that you?"

"Yes." I exhaled. "I'm at the bridge, ready to cross."

"Please hurry." Fear tainted her voice.

"Keep a close watch on Frank. Don't let him out of your sight," I said and then added, "I'll find her."

My words were steadier than my thoughts. Frank might have lied about Ashley's whereabouts. Even if the girl was in the church, she could have managed to get loose. Given the mindset of people on the streets, she'd be in danger.

"Eddie?" Beth cut in. "Be careful."

"I'll call you back soon." Clicking off the radio, I stuffed it in my pocket and moved on.

A dead traffic light, hung from a post that led across the bridge, swayed in the wind. Abandoned cars sat idle on the overpass.

Remaining out of sight while crossing the bridge would be impossible. Unlike the town with its deserted houses, trees and cars, hiding places were sparse. If I ran into anyone who had a gun and an attitude, I'd be an open target. However, nobody came and I crossed the bridge without incident.

While less in the open than on the bridge, the houses thinned considerably on the other side of town. I'd be easily spotted by unwanted eyes. Turning up North Street, I hoofed it through alleys and side streets. Just around the corner of Mulligan's Laundromat, I found myself standing in front of the large stone structure of Saint Jude's. The door of the church stood slightly ajar. I gave it a push and it creaked open. Puffing cold mist into my hands, I stepped inside.

Even after weeks of sitting in frigid temperatures, the place smelled like the Sistine Chapel. Incense that burned for decades still lingered in the walls.

I pulled out my radio. "Beth?"

"Eddie?" A nervous pause. "Did you find her?"

"Not yet. I just got here. I'm gonna have a look around."

"Please hurry." Quiet desperation crawled over Beth's words.

Clicking the radio off, I continued on.

I turned on my flashlight and shined it around. White doves were painted on the ceiling of the vestibule and a small bench with a stack of church bulletins sat near the front door. Portraits of ministers, perhaps over a hundred years old, lined the walls.

Swallowing cold air, I moved slowly down the corridor. My footsteps echoed in the silent and dark hall as if walking in a tomb amongst long dead kings.

Near the end of the corridor there was a room filled with tables. Paper plates and empty plastic cups sat on placemats, perhaps in preparation for a church social, or in another scenario, a Sunday night AA meeting where reformed drinkers bolstered their strength against the evils of the bottle. The thought occurred to me that at least alcoholics could rival in the idea that distilleries were shutdown nationwide. Booze was becoming extinct and backsliding wouldn't be an option.

"Ashley?" I said.

Nobody answered.

Turning left, I walked through a wooden door that led into the worship area. Pictures of Jesus graced the walls and a baptismal fountain stood at the base of the church. Rows of empty pews led to the pulpit and a tarnished cross on the altar.

A tipped over communion chalice lay on the red carpet in front of the choir loft.

As a kid I served as an acolyte in one of the local churches. After services, the minister would take the acolytes to the Sunrise Diner for a couple of eggs and greasy bacon. It wasn't a feast for kings, but hell, at the time it tasted better than lobster and white wine.

Church had its boring moments. Still it was a good memory. To this day when I close my eyes, I can hear my mother, dressed in a white choir gown, singing hymns and praises on Sunday mornings. But standing in the sunken darkness that the world had become, even a sanctuary like church, once comforting and warm, looked somehow alien.

Looking around, stone statues of Apostles stood near a bed of wilted flowers by the communion table. Staring at the sculptures, a chill, colder than Arctic winds, crawled down my backbone. It wasn't nostalgia or memories that gave me a shiver. It's what I saw surrounding the altar.

All the candles were lit.

"Eddie? My heart jumped at the sound of Beth's voice on the radio.

"Right here," I answered.

"Did you find anything?"

I paused and stared at the flickering candlelight. Shining my flashlight around, I didn't see anyone. At the same time, marble statues didn't crawl off the pedestals and light the candles. Somebody was here. I couldn't relinquish that information to Beth. She'd get frightened; bolt out of the house and across town to the church. That'd be dangerous. Not to mention, Frank was tied to a post, struggling to break free.

"Nothing so far," I lied. "I'm checking the rooms. Call you back soon." I quickly stuffed the radio back in my pocket.

Looking from side to side, the beam of the flashlight danced over empty pews like grave markers in a cemetery.

"Is anyone here?" My voice echoed in the dark.

I stopped to listen and heard a noise. It came from somewhere near the altar. I could see a wooden door behind the choir stall, possibly a dressing room or a rector's office.

"Help," a frail voice sounded out, barely audible.

"Ashley?" My heart beat faster.

Walking up the center aisle, I turned my head suspiciously from side to side. There was no telling who was abroad. I grabbed a candlestick that had been posted alongside one of the pews and held it out in front of me like a sword.

"Help!"

This time the voice was followed by the thump of a fist against a wall or a door.

Racing over to the door, I jiggled the handle. It was locked tight.

"Ashley?"

"I'm in here," she cried. "Please help."

"Don't worry. I'm gonna get you out."

The question was how? This wasn't a movie. A battering ram wouldn't mysteriously turn up underneath a church pew. If I wanted to get in, I'd need to break the door down.

Standing there thinking about it, who could have ever imagined any of this? I was a car salesman from northeast Pennsylvania whose diet consisted of donuts and industrial strength coffee. Now, a few weeks later, I took to looting churches and smashing down doors in the dead of night.

"Keep away from the entrance, understand?"

Bracing myself, I charged forward and hit the door. It buckled but didn't break. Crashing into it again produced the same results.

"Remember what your football coach used to tell you? Hit that freaking hole like a man, you little snot!" said the voice in my head again. The guy grew to be a real pain in the ass, but at least he was an inspirational one.

Kicking my feet against the carpet and lowering my shoulder, I ran headfirst towards the door but abruptly stopped.

Just across the aisle on the far side of the altar, something moved. Shining my flashlight, green eyes glinted. At first I thought it might be an animal, but it seemed much too large, even for a big dog like Shadow. Quickly veering off to the left, the dark figure crouched behind the church organ.

"Hello?" I searched the darkness.

If silence were a lake, I would have drowned in the stillness of the water.

Slow but deliberate, a woman stood up. Her ragged breath spilled out and echoed against the walls of the church. My eyes widened when I saw the knife. The edge of the blade gleamed in the flickering candlelight as she stood poised to strike.

23

Dead Pools

When I was young, I had an aunt who lived across the alley. She worked in a sewing machine factory years prior to the government sending all of our jobs to China. In later life, those golden years, she started to become forgetful. Little things like hairdresser appointments or where she put the house keys slipped her mind. I thought it was just part of the aging process. That changed on a warm but breezy September night when the phone rang.

"Hello?"

"Eddie?"

Raising an eyebrow I glanced at the clock. It was 3:00 in the morning. "Who is this?"

"Doris Henley. I live over on Pine."

"Is something wrong?"

"You need to come to your aunt's house." Her voice sounded rushed and worried. "She's not well."

Thinking the worst, I threw on a tee shirt and jeans then hurried across the alley into my aunt's house.

Aunt Annie sat on the couch and paged through a telephone directory, her face glossed over in confusion.

"She came to my door about an hour ago," Doris whispered. "She's looking for Tom."

I sat down beside my aunt on the couch. "Aunt Annie? Is something wrong?"

"It's Tom," she said, a worried look in her eye. "We were talking and went up to bed a few hours ago. When I woke up, he was gone. Just gone!" A tear slipped down her cheek. "I'm scared and don't know who to call."

I wasn't used to seeing my aunt this way. Aunt Annie made people laugh all of her life. She didn't need a winning lottery ticket or a Caribbean cruise. A Bogart movie on a Saturday night and an occasional sip of Harvey's Bristol Cream made her smile. But things in her world started to change. She began to forget. She began to drift.

"Aunt Annie." I took her hand and softly said, "Uncle Tom is gone. He died ten years ago."

She tilted her head and looked at me as if I were crazy. "Don't you think I know that?" she said. "But he was sitting here a few hours ago, talking to me as if he never left." She pointed at his easy chair where he watched the Sunday afternoon football games. "He told me he loved me and that it was time to go home." She paused. "My mother was with him too. I know." Tears glistened on her cheeks. "You think I'm crazy."

At near ninety, Aunt Annie's eyes were still bright as a teenager in love. Lately dementia had taken root, but even with that dreaded disease, I still believed her. She was approaching the bridge on her last journey in life and perhaps already had a foot in the next world. If she saw things and believed that they were real, who was I to disagree?

Whatever the circumstance, Aunt Annie wasn't herself. Lines of age crystallized underneath her eyes. She was still the sweet woman who made me cocoa as a kid, only now, haunted by visions of the dead roamed the halls of her house.

"Can't you see them?" She stared at empty space and pointed with trembling fingers.

I didn't see them. I didn't see anything, but I did remember the ghosted look that fell across her frozen expression like the fine mist of a dark storm.

Now, years later, as I stood by an altar confronting a woman guarding a pulpit with a butcher knife, I saw that same troubled look that once occupied my Aunt Annie's disintegrating world. But dissimilar from my aunt who stayed happy in the days that remained, the woman in the church glared with contempt that illuminated every fierce corner of her unordinary world.

Unlike Aunt Annie, his one was dangerous.

"Go away." The woman held tight to the knife. "You're not welcome here."

Italian and perhaps once beautiful, she had piercing dark eyes and a smudge of grime dirtied her cheek. Long hair, matted and splashed with grey, enveloped her face. She stared at me from underneath layers of tattered clothes and fingerless mittens.

"Gina Grace?" I blinked in the darkness. "Is that you?"

She glared fiercely at me. "I said go away!"

I remembered Gina, at least vaguely. She was a waitress down at Molly Spirits, a cocktail lounge over on Hamilton. On Thursdays I rolled in there after work to grab a beer and hot wings. Dressed in black slacks and a pullover Molly Spirit's tee-shirt, Gina had a killer smile and the face of an angel. The drama of the oil famine changed those particulars. In the sunken glow of candlelight and cold stone walls of an abandoned church, only a shadow of the woman remained. Warding off freezing temperatures and scouring trashcans for half eaten hot dogs does that to a person every time.

"Don't you remember me?" I asked, keeping the candlestick firmly out in front of me. "Molly Spirits, right? I'm Eddie Slate."

Gina's head tilted suspiciously. For an instant a fog of confusion seemed to lift from her eyes but just as quickly settled back over her thoughts. "I know what you want." She pointed from one side of the altar to the other. "We all know."

I scratched my head and looked around. "Is someone else here?"

"The Lord, of course," she said smartly, the knife bolted tight in her hand.

Looking in her unbalanced eyes, you'd swear someone pulled out a big black magic marker and scribbled the word *DEMENTIA* all over her face. No doubt a lack of food and a tainted past helped to open the bridge to madness.

A few years back it was in all the local newspapers. Gina, a single mother, had a daughter named Angeline. One bright sunny morning the kid had been playing down by Foster's Pond. Later that day, Gina found her floating in stagnant water in what the locals later referred to as The Dead Pool. There was no time to prepare, resolve any misunderstandings or even say goodbye. Angeline drowned.

The news hit Gina with all the weight of an eighteen wheel rig. She suffered a nervous breakdown and tried desperately to pick up the pieces of her shattered life. After a time she started working at Molly Spirits as a waitress. She even began smiling again, at least halfheartedly.

Until now, that is.

"I don't want any trouble." I took a step back. "I'm looking for a little girl."

"A girl?" Gina glanced at the closed door behind the choir stall and then shifted back to me. "He told me I could keep her."

"Who told you?"

"The man who left her here."

A vision of Frank flashed across my mind. His dark influence, a broken sewer pipe, flowed down the gutters and through the front door of a church, into the hands of a mad woman.

"I'm warning you." The knife trembled in Gina's fingers. "Go away. You'll never take my daughter."

"Your daughter?" I blinked in confusion.

"I'll kill her before I let you have her. I'll kill both of us."

"You're not thinking straight Gina." I took a step towards her. "You lost your daughter years ago, remember? Her name was Angeline, right? I read about it in the newspapers. It happened at Foster's Pond. Nobody expects you to get over a thing like that. It was a tragedy, but the girl in there?" I pointed at the closed door behind the choir stall. "She needs her mother."

"I am her mother!" Hot coals glowed in Gina's eyes.

"I'm telling you, you're not. She belongs to someone else."

Craters of doubt sunk into Gina's expression. A distant look of remorse, echoes in the haunting wind, filled her face. After a frozen instant, her head jerked sideways, almost as if she received a cold slap on the cheek.

"You're a liar!" Her fierce gaze and accusing finger pointed in my direction.

Without warning, Gina let out a loud scream and lunged towards me with the knife.

24

A Crazy Little Thing like You

Gina Grace, no, check that... not Gina Grace. The attractive waitress from Molly Spirits left the house. A woman with fiery eyes, crazy eyes, infiltrated her body. Knocking over a pot of dead poinsettias that sat on a table next to the altar, she charged forward.

A person like Frank might have been amused at the call to combat. He would have painted on an alligator grin and then broke her neck, leaving her to expire on the carpet in the icy chill of winter. The thing is, I'm not Frank. I didn't have the killer instinct. Thoughts of engaging in a good old fashioned fist fight terrified me, let alone a raging mad woman with a dagger.

"Devil!" Gina slashed the knife against empty air.

Stumbling backward, I swung the candlestick. It hit her shoulder and jarred the knife loose from her hand. The weapon skidded across the floor and came to an abrupt halt against a church pew. Whirling around, the woman slammed an elbow hard into my neck, leaving me gasping for air. She followed up with a firm kick to the mid section and then another to the side of my jaw. My head snapped back and I fell to the floor.

"You want to take my baby?" She shouted wildly. Stooping down, she picked up the knife and waved it frantically in my face. "You'll never take her alive."

Marching over to the room behind the choir stall, she pulled a key from her pocket and unlocked the door. Reaching in, she pulled Ashley out by a tuft of hair and dragged her to the altar.

Pushing myself up on bruised elbows, I quickly got to my feet. I stood there frozen. What was I supposed to do? I wasn't a hostage negotiator or an overpriced psychologist ready to solve the world's emotional malfunctions with a prescription for Prozac. I was just a car salesman trying to stay alive on a hostile planet.

Ashley's chin trembled and her terrified eyes flooded with tears.

"Don't do this." I gripped the top of a pew. "We can get you help Gina."

"Help?" The woman's laugh echoed through the church. "There is no help for us out here." A lonely wind moaned outside the building. "Ask them." She looked around. "Ask all of them."

"Nobody else is here Gina. You're hallucinating."

"Are you insane?" She slapped her forehead in disbelief. "They're all around us!" She pointed at invisible forces that festered in the confines of her own diseased mind.

"I'm telling you, there's nobody here. Please Gina, give me the girl."

"Never."

"Give her to me!" I pounded a fist on the pew.

Gina's lips curled up in rage. "You can bury her!" She raised the knife.

Ashley screamed. In the last pivotal second, she wriggled free of her captor's grip and ran behind the pulpit.

Gina's green eyes sparkled madly in the glow of candlelight. Bolting from the altar and sheathed by darkness, the woman disappeared behind one of the pews.

My heart beating hard, I looked around uncertainly. "Ashley?" I whispered. "Where are you?"

I could hear someone breathing in the shadows.

"Ashley. Come out. I won't hurt you."

Suddenly Gina materialized from beside the church's pulpit, inches from me and slashing the knife wildly in stagnant air. I grabbed her arm and banged it off the side wall. She dropped the knife but accelerated the assault. Jumping on my back, she gouged at my eyes.

"Let go!" I swung around and tried to loosen her grip.

Gina's bony fingers dug into my throat. I stumbled backward against a partition near a staircase at the top of the vestibule. Loosening her grip, Gina let go and lost her balance. She tumbled headfirst down the flight of stairs and came to rest at the bottom with a heavy thud.

In the haunting silence, I walked slowly down the staircase. At the bottom, her limbs twisted, Gina Grace breathed in short raspy gasps. She stared up at the ceiling. A single tear weaved down her cheek. A minute later, she slipped away.

Kneeling down beside the woman, I thought about her life. Gina's love for her daughter was like petals of lilacs in a windy green field that would color the meadow long after her passing. Even in a tragic world, I'd like to believe she found peace. I needed to believe that. I also needed to believe that same daughter she found one sad morning at Foster's Pond would be waiting for her in the next world, glowing of smiles, as she fell into the arms of her mother. I needed to believe that because standing there in a place without innocence or mercy, I needed to know that there was still some shred of light shining in the world. I needed to know that someday, somewhere, there would be a sunrise. Brushing my hand over Gina's face, I closed her eyes.

Maybe it was lack of sleep or frayed nerves but in that tragic moment, I wept like a baby.

"Mister?" I heard a voice behind me.

Wiping my nose on a sleeve, I turned around.

Ashley stood behind me. Her ashen complexion was muddied with tears. Trembling, she opened her arms and put them around me.

That instant of despair might have been the closest thing I'd ever know to having a kid. I used to take my niece miniature golfing and to an occasional concert. But when it came to being a dad, I didn't stand tall in terms of experience. Still I'm telling you, feeling that little girl's arms around me and her tears on my neck? I grew ten feet in less than a minute.

"It's gonna be okay." I swallowed hard.

"Really?" She sniffed.

I smiled weakly.

Who was I kidding? Probably not an eight year old; they're smarter than that. Maybe someday civilization would crawl off its knees and stand up again. Businesses might reopen and high school football games would be played on Saturday afternoons, but not today. Today the only saving grace on the planet was a semi-automatic or a good solid club.

"Please don't leave me mister." Ashley snuffled, her nose running. Fear washed over her like a pool of murky water.

"Don't worry. I'm here to help." And I was. Even if it turned out to be the last thing I ever did, I was gonna save this kid. I'd keep her out of harm's way.

Pulling the radio out of my pocket, I flicked it on. "Beth, are you copying me?" Nothing but dead static. I tapped the transmitter on my hand. "Beth, are you listening? I found her. I found Ashley. She's safe. Beth?" More empty static. "Are you there?"

After a minute, the static cleared. "It sounds like you had a busy day cowboy," a grungy voice answered.

My blood iced up. "Frank?"

"Don't sound so surprised," he said. "Take a piece of advice. If you want to be a Boy Scout, learn how to tie a knot."

My jaw dropped. I stared blankly at the radio. The bastard got loose.

"Where's Beth?"

"Indisposed."

"Let her go Frank."

"Sorry, I can't do that."

"You win," I conceded. "I'll give you all my food, supplies, everything. Just let Beth go."

"You're not getting it, are you?" Frank laughed. "You crossed the line Eddie. You got in my way. I can't let something like that go unpunished. Someone has to pay for that. Someone has to die."

I heard Beth moan in the background. "Touch her and I'll kill you." I clenched my fists.

"Still trying to be a hero? I'll tell you what," Frank said. "Let's make a deal."

"A deal?"

"Call it a momentary stay of execution."

"You're crazy."

"According to my psych evaluation at the prison, yes," Frank concurred.

"What do you want from me?"

"Remember the old high school?" He paused. "Man, we had some laughs there, right?"

I remembered the school well. Back then Frank had already been groomed to spend a fruitless life in the state pen before he ever reached his sixteenth birthday. Guys like him?

They busted people up for sheer amusement. I was one of those kids, horn-rimmed taped glasses and silver braces. Frank fancied himself a boxer and spent his wasted youth using faces like mine for a punching bag.

"Meet me at the school in an hour," said Frank.

"Why?"

"We got unfinished business."

"I'm not meeting you anywhere."

"It's your choice cowboy, but if you're a minute longer than an hour?" Frank paused. "I'll cut off one of Beth's fingers. Two minutes, I take out an eye. After ten minutes, don't bother rushing. You can pick up her pieces in an apple cart."

"Don't hurt her," I ordered.

"That's up to you Eddie. You got the power."

Pausing, I finally said, "I'll be there."

"Great. It'll be one hell of a reunion, right?" Frank said. "And Eddie?"

"What?"

"I found the bullets you were looking for in the upstairs closet. By the way," he said. "Nice red fedora."

The transmission went dead and the radio filled with static.

25

Alma Mater

I used to spend summers in Ocean City, a beach town in Maryland. There's something about the boardwalk and crashing waves that made me feel invincible. One year Hurricane Charlie made landfall during my stay. Rain poured down in buckets and brilliant streaks of lightning painted the sky.

"That was a rough vacation. I walked through a hurricane," I'd later tell my friends.

Now, thirty days after the world's oil supply bellied up, I was walking into a hurricane again, only this time instead of Charlie, the monster's name was Frank.

"Is my mom in trouble?" Ashley asked fearfully.

"It's gonna be okay." Bending down, I ruffled her hair. Judging by the look on Ashley's face, my voice held about as much confidence as a boxer who just took an uppercut in the twelfth and went down on the rug.

It was no secret; Frank wanted to lure me into a trap. Even a car salesman could see that. I didn't comply with the rules of the game and now he wanted payback.

Glancing down at Ashley, the kid posed another problem. If I met Frank for a showdown, what would I do with her? I couldn't leave her alone while I stormed off on a suicide mission. Vagrants wandered the streets. She'd be easy prey.

"Please mister." Ashley tugged on my sleeve. "I want to go home."

A twinge ran through my heart. The kid may have been too green around the ears to realize it, but these days? Home was no more attainable than finding a lush green mountain in the middle of the Sahara.

About a week or so ago I went outside on a recon mission, down by Gilmore's flower shop, searching for food and supplies. I found a woman, thirties, bundled in an L.L.Bean jacket. She was curled up in a gutter under an awning at Mallard's Roadside Bar. A purple scarf had been wrapped tight around her throat. It's unclear how she met her fate, but with no fuel to gas up the backhoes to dig a grave, she'd likely be fermenting in the streets until the spring thaw. Life wasn't pretty and getting uglier all the time.

"You don't look so good mister." Ashley squeezed her hands together.

I forced a grin, but I was far from okay. It wasn't just Frank or the heartbreak of watching the world fall to pieces. After so many days in the trenches, I became desensitized. A month ago getting a paper cut in the office sent me running to the doctor for a tetanus shot. These days I've learned to ignore the spectacle of a corpse in a gutter. It happens to soldiers in war. See enough of the bad stuff and sooner or later it'll make you numb inside.

Still something in that little girl, her big blue eyes staring at me, jarred my heart. For the first time in a month a sense of something innocent washed over me. Ashley needed me to survive. I wouldn't let her down.

"Listen close," I told the girl. "You're gonna have to do everything I say. Do you understand?"

Ashley sheepishly nodded her head. "Are you gonna find my mom?"

Staring at her, I smiled but said nothing. That was the question of the day.

Slipping out of the church, we headed into the streets. We moved along back roads and alleys, silent as the grave. Garbed in beat up sneakers and a jacket two sizes too big, Ashley struggled to keep up the pace. I picked her up and carried her across 10th Avenue, passed the old Olympian Drive In, a once popular hot spot for local teens. Wiping a smudge off my wristwatch, I checked the time.

It was 2:32 a.m.

"Where are we going?" Ashley stared out into the gloom. "Are we gonna find her?" she asked. "Are we gonna find my mom?"

I kept moving without answering. How could I? Desperate situations changed faster than the snap of a finger. Frank would be waiting in ambush. In the end, I'd be the mouse driven to the cheese.

Only yesterday, outside of stealing a gallon of kerosene or digging a stale donut out of a trashcan, nothing mattered. Frank singlehandedly changed the dynamics of that circumstance with a stupid little hand radio, and for all I knew, Beth was already dead.

Crossing the road, I walked down Asphalt Street. The high school came into full view. Half of the classroom windows were broken by vandals. A lopsided sign hung above the main entrance of the school that read, *"Home of the OLYMPIANS"* in bold letters. Yellow school buses, their windows frosty from the night air, lined the side of the building.

Even now, caught up in disaster, roaming the school halls seemed like yesterday. Boys became men and girls turned into effeminate women. Young freshman with button down shirts had fear written in their eyes as they struggled against a stampede of juniors and seniors. There were homecoming queens, prom kings, pimple cream and wallflowers on weekend dances.

Now here I was again, years later, standing in front of my old alma mater. Only this time instead of doodling on a history notebook or ogling a Spanish teacher with a brilliant smile that looked like Cameron Diaz, I'm at odds with a killer.

The front door of the school stood ajar; so much for security measures against terroristic threats. Stepping inside, I shined my flashlight around. The dull beam glinted off lockers that lined the halls. Principal Skinner's office was the first door on the right. Taking Ashley by the hand, we slipped inside.

Papers and detention slips were strewn on the principal's desk. A picture of Skinner's wife and son had fallen off the wall and a trashcan, tipped over. Otherwise, the room showed no signs of forced entry.

Bending down I whispered to Ashley, "Stay here. Keep out of sight. If anyone comes, hide." I pointed underneath a desk. "Got it?"

"You won't leave me here." Ashley shivered.

"Don't worry," I told her. "It'll be okay, but if for some reason I couldn't make it back..."

"You have to make it back." Frightened, Ashley grabbed my arm.

Dread painted the kid's eyes; still I needed to prepare her in case the worst happened.

Reaching in a pocket I pulled out my wallet. Amazing, right? The world had all the chaos of a nuclear attack and I still carried around credit cards and a discount ticket for a McDonald's Happy Meal.

"Take this." I handed her my driver's license. "If I'm not back in twenty minutes, go to this address." I pointed at the license. "I'll meet you there. It's just across town by the Diligent Firehouse. Stay on the backstreets. Be careful not to let anyone see you. You're a smart kid." I ruffled her hair. "You can do this."

"I don't know." Ashley's voice grew shaky. She pulled and twisted her shirt.

"There's food and bottled water in the house," I told her. "It's upstairs in the attic underneath some loose floorboards. Search around. You'll find it." I wiped a tear off her cheek with my knuckle.

Sniffing, she reached out and hugged me. "Please come back mister," she whispered in my ear.

I'm gonna give it to you straight. My heart shattered like glass on cement when I looked in that kid's face. She should have been playing with dolls and jumping rope in the backyard. Then the lights went out and the world turned dark. She lost her mother, her family, her life. And now she was in danger of losing me.

I'd come back. Even if it meant walking through fire I'd come back. The trouble is Frank had another agenda. One of us was going to die. If things went bad, Ashley would be alone and left to fend for herself. A candle in a windstorm, the light would be snuffed out.

Pulling out the principal's chair, I prodded Ashley to crawl underneath the desk. Curling up in a ball, she tucked her hands around her knees and quietly rocked in the darkness.

Turning my flashlight off, I stepped into the hall. Except for moonlight in the windows, the corridor was a grey and filled with shadows.

Tiptoeing down the corridor, I turned left towards the cafeteria. The scent of rotted meat and sour milk lingered in the air, no doubt spoiled provisions turned moldy over the last few weeks since classes let out in lieu of the oil shortage.

I guessed that the school might have been used as a sanctuary in the days following the disaster. People could still be holed up in the boiler room, but if they were, other than rodents scurrying the halls, there were no signs of survivors.

My heart jumped at the abrupt sound of static clearing on the radio.

"Hey Eddie, you with me cowboy?" said Frank. "I'm waiting for you."

I stared at the radio and swallowed hard. It was show time.

26

The Faceoff

"You hear me cowboy?" Frank said again. "Pick up."

I raised the radio to my lips. "Yeah, right here Frank."

"Did you bring your lunch money?" He sniggered like a teenager. "We got a lot on the menu tonight."

I glanced up and down the hall. There was no movement. That didn't give me much comfort. It was dark. Frank could be standing in front of me with a butcher knife, an inch from my throat, and I wouldn't even know it.

"Where are you?" I demanded. "Let's get this over with."

"Patience," Frank advised. "You'll find me soon enough." He paused and whistled. "Man, time flies. You remember going to school here? I kicked the shit out of you more than once in the halls. The good old days, right?"

I didn't answer. He was trying to get underneath my skin. Make me afraid. Still he remained careful and tolerant. A lion in the jungle, Frank would pounce when the moment was right.

"You can still run," said the voice in my head. *"Don't be stupid. Grab the kid. Bolt for the door and disappear into the darkness."*

The problem was that Frank held Beth captive. Her increasingly grim fate depended on my actions.

A flood of guilt engulfed me. If I hadn't mentioned her name on the radio, she'd be tucked away in her house, wrapped in blankets and waiting for help to arrive with food and supplies.

I kept walking.

Near the end of the hall, I passed room 106, my old English class. The teacher's name was Alberta Klein, a short stocky woman with an overbite and horn-rimmed glasses. I used to write these stupid poems in her class. Ha! Poems, what the hell was that? Mrs. Klein liked them though. She thought I had a future in writing. She'd say, "Keep up the great work Eddie. Someday you'll be the next Walt Whitman." Unfortunately those melodic verses that touched her soul wouldn't do me much good right about now. I needed a shotgun and a good aim.

"Enjoying the nostalgia?" Frank's voice on the radio startled me. "Keep alert," he warned. "You can never tell when you'll take a bullet to the back of the head."

"What's wrong Frank, afraid to show yourself?"

"Keep talking cowboy." He laughed. "Just keep talkin'."

Turning down a corridor, I walked towards the gymnasium. A door stood open at the entrance of the field house. Still Frank was conspicuously absent. I started to wonder if he might be broadcasting from another location leaving me to mindlessly chase long dead ghosts and memories.

"You're getting warm," said Frank. "Don't give up the hunt."

"Stop playing games," I told him. "Where are you?"

"I wouldn't be so anxious. You could be dead in the next ten minutes," he reminded.

Approaching the gymnasium entrance, my feet stopped. I heard a noise inside, quiet as a soft footed cat. I picked up a football trophy that sat on a mantel in the foyer. If nothing else, it'd serve as a solid blunt object for defense. Gripping it tight, I stepped through the entry door of the gym.

Inside, a half deflated basketball had been kicked against the bleachers and pom poms were tossed on the floor. A large mural of a baseball player that said *GO OLYMPIANS* hung on the wall.

Another noise, this time to the right of me, came from inside a locker room. Stepping over to it, I put my ear against the door. Someone shuffled around in there; the natives were restless.

I had no idea what fate awaited me. More than likely it'd be a blade driven through my throat or a gunshot to the back of the head. Still I needed to survive. I needed to conquer. Beth's future depended on it. Her daughter Ashley, hidden under a desk, no doubt would suffer a similar destiny if Frank wasn't stopped.

Taking a deep breath, I opened the door and stepped in.

It was dark and I couldn't see anything. Even though the place hadn't been used in weeks, stale sweat, the odor of kids running laps around the basketball court or pounding out yardage on the football field, lingered in the air.

"Frank?" My fingers gripped the brass trophy that I found in the foyer.

After a moment, an answer came, not by radio, but rather the dull thud of a bullet landing in a tin locker. I gasped and quickly retreated to the rear of the room.

"What took you so long?" The distinctive sound of my nemesis echoed in the aisles.

"What do you want from me?" I asked.

"That's a stupid question. We got issues, don't you think?" said Frank. "I don't like playing the fool. That's what you did cowboy. You played me. Crap like that gets people killed every day."

I couldn't pinpoint Frank's position. Judging by the direction of his voice, he was somewhere near the front of the room.

"Are you listening?" Frank fired off another round. It ricocheted off the wall and buried itself in a shower stall. "Show yourself."

"What, so you can kill me?"

"We all die sometime, right? It's just a question of when and how."

Other than the door where I entered, there was no viable means of escape. Noise also posed a problem. Even the tap of a shoe would be sufficient to give Frank enough of a target to take a shot.

I saw a shadow move near a window in the front of the room. Frank was close. Still disarming him would prove impossible. He'd be on top of me before I got three feet. I needed a diversion.

"You gonna hide like a pigeon in a hole all night?" Frank asked. "I did a stint in Afghanistan some years after graduation," he said. "The enemy hid in sand mounds. We had to fish them out of the dunes with explosives. I liked blowing things up, but it really pissed me off, you know? I hated the desert. You can bet your ass I really made them suffer for the inconvenience. Is that what you want Eddie, for me to make you suffer? Trust me," he said. "Before I'm done, you'll beg for a bullet in a firing squad."

Frank wouldn't wait much longer to exact his brand of justice. I needed to hit him hard. Fast. If I could derail his concentration, even for a few seconds, I might be able to get close enough to take him out.

"Are you ignoring me?" The hammer on his gun clicked again. "Damn-it, show some respect."

Holding my breath, I abruptly flung the brass trophy across the room. It landed in the next row, clattering loudly against the lockers.

Turning quickly, Frank pivoted to the left and fired off a quick round. The bullet hit the wall with a hard clunk.

That was the crucial moment. I raced up the aisle. Frank turned. I struck his arm as he squeezed off a shot. The bullet landed in the ceiling. The oomph of a bony knee to the kidneys was enough to have him drop the gun. Hitting the ground fast and hard, I scooped it up, rolled over and fired at will.

It was a hit. Frank groaned, clutched his shoulder and staggered against a locker. Stumbling over to the exit, he flung the door open and slipped outside.

"Don't stop now, you stupid son of a bitch," the frantic voice in my head shouted. *"If he escapes, Beth is dead and he'll never stop hunting you. The fox is on the run. Finish the job before he recovers."*

Holding tight to the rifle, I quickly got to my feet and hurried out the door.

Turning down the hall, I instantly saw a moving shadow trudge up the corridor.

"Frank! Stop or I'll shoot."

Discounting my warning, he continued moving towards the school's exit door.

"Are you listening?" I aimed the gun. "I said stop!"

Fingering a wounded shoulder, Frank abruptly turned around. A stiff grin played on his lips. "What are you going to do cowboy, take me out?"

"Just give me Beth. We'll call it a day," I told him. "You go your way, I'll go mine."

Grinning, he took a step forward.

"Don't test me Frank," I kept the rifle glued on his eyes. "Where's Beth?"

"Pull that trigger and you'll never find out." He glanced at the exit.

"You're running out of time," I warned.

"I think you're bluffing."

The thing is I wasn't bluffing. The meek car salesman with the spiffy shoes and red tie had been tossed to the ghetto, an unprincipled victim of the system. I was prepared to kill. Even if Beth was alive, Frank would never tell me where he had her. He'd stall for time, wait for an opening and then snap my neck at the first opportunity.

"You'll have to kill me." He stared me down.

I raised the rifle. "It's the end of the rainbow Frank. Say goodbye."

A portrait of doubt painted Frank's expression. His face turned into a staring eye as I started to squeeze the trigger.

Unfortunately, that was the instant fate stepped in the corridor and arrived in the form of a frightened little eight year old girl.

Ashley raced around the corner of the foyer and came to a sudden stop in the middle of the hall. Jolted at her arrival, my finger froze on the trigger.

"Ashley!" I shouted. "Get back!"

Too late.

Frank swooped in. He trapped the girl under his forearm and picked her up. Holding her in front of him like a human shield, he pulled out a knife and put it to her throat.

"Drop the gun."

"That isn't gonna happen Frank." I held tight to my target.

"Drop it or she dies!" The edge of the blade tickled the underside of Ashley's chin.

A mountain of fear sprouted up on Ashley's face. Her tears glistened like icy branches in a winter storm. "I'm sorry mister," she said. "I got scared. Please. Don't let him hurt me."

"Listen to the kid Eddie," Frank yanked Ashley's head back and further explored her throat with the tip of the blade. "You want her blood on your hands?"

Even in a compromised situation, one in which Ashley's life stood in doubt, I couldn't relinquish my last line of defense. If I lowered the gun, Frank would kill us both.

"It's simple Frank." I pointed the rifle and played the cards. "If you hurt her, I kill you, got it?"

The dormant air of the abandoned schoolhouse flared in my nostrils and expelled from my lungs in frosty and rapid puffs. My aim remained fixed on Frank, solid as a deadbolt.

Frank tilted his head uncertainly. "It looks like we got ourselves a faceoff."

"Let her go Frank."

"Not gonna happen. The kid is collateral." He stepped towards the exit.

I glanced down at a bloodstain on his shirt where I grazed him with a bullet in the locker room. "I shot you once. You really think I won't finish the job?"

"That was a lucky bullet. Not to mention, I didn't have a kid obstructing the central target." Frank glanced at the gun trembling in my hands. "My guess is that you never won any trophies in a duck shoot, but if you really want to fire? Be careful. You could kill the wrong person." He held Ashley firmly in front of him.

My finger remained iced up on the trigger. Frank was right. I didn't spend my time plugging clay ducks at the local range. I had a terrible aim.

"Here's the deal," Frank announced, beaming with confidence. "I'm going out that door cowboy, and if you follow me?" He shook Ashley hard. "I'll kill the brat. I'll do more than kill her. I'll tie her up in the woods for the wolves. Even they're hungry these days."

Ashley stared at me through pleading eyes. Her sobs echoed in the school's empty halls.

Taking another step, Frank pushed open the side exit door. "Remember," he warned. "Keep your distance." Grinning smartly, he slipped outside, into the night.

Disregarding threats, I rushed out the door after Frank with the gun poised to fire. However, outside of the wind, the streets were empty and secretive.

Frank was gone.

27

Where for art thou Frank

I walked the streets for hours. On Broadway, I passed Wong's takeout restaurant. Someone spray painted some graffiti on the side of the building that said, *ALL DEAD HERE*. An abandoned green Chevy with a flat tire, the driver's door flung open, sat in the middle of an intersection by the courthouse. No kids stood on crosswalks waiting for school buses and the lottery numbers posted on Dugan's storefront window were forever frozen in time.

Looking around, houses lined both sides of the street. Frank could have been holed up in any of them. Hope of Beth and Ashley's rescue faded as certainly as the sun behind a dark mountainside. I had no idea where to start looking.

"Hey buddy." A vagrant wearing a quilted jacket and sneakers called to me from in front of JT's Bar. "You got a spare cigarette?"

I didn't answer. I didn't trust him. I didn't trust anyone. These days, good people had wilted away like flowers in the dead of winter. Tucking my head down, I kept walking.

Tired and cold, after awhile I sat down on a curb outside of Danny's Carnival Supplies. My eyes stung as if someone poured salt in them. A high octane caffeine fix from Starbucks would have done miracles.

Pulling out my radio, I pushed the talk button. "Frank, you still out there?"

If Frank was listening, he maintained radio silence. I did, however, hear a strange noise in the background. Something tingled like chimes. I couldn't pinpoint the source but knew that I heard the sound before.

Rubbing my knees, I stood up and trudged down an alley. If I hoped to find Beth and Ashley, time needed to be measured in minutes rather than hours. Still I couldn't continue without any rest.

Reaching my house, I slipped back inside to the cellar lifestyle that I had become accustomed to. The place looked quiet and deserted.

"Shadow?" I whistled up the cellar steps but heard no thump of paws on the carpet. Frank had either chased the dog off, or in a grimmer scenario, put a bullet in his head. Either way, there were no signs of the animal.

I was alone.

Jagged lines of tension cut across my forehead but despite the stress, my eyes closed quickly. I'm not sure how long I laid there but I'm certain I dreamed of happier times. There were shopping malls and movie theaters. Long drives on lazy summer days and romantic walks by the ocean under the stars.

I dreamed about living again.

When I woke up, I hoped it was all just nightmare. I hoped to hear the hum of the electric grid or maybe a television set. Instead of the darkness of a damp and cold house, CNN would be reporting on a rare butterfly in the Amazon about to go extinct or Donald Trump would be pissed off about something and running for president again. But that didn't happen. When my eyes blinked open, I was curled up on the floor of a dank cellar and the only sound I heard was the chimes on the radio.

"Well cowboy, you just had to be a hero, and where did it get you?" Frank's voice again cracked the airwaves. "Beth's gone. Ashley vanished. You're alone."

Raising my head off the floor, I looked around suspiciously. The thought occurred to me that Frank might have sneaked back inside the house while I slept and could be watching me. If he was, I'd never see the knife fall.

"What did you do with them Frank?" I asked. "Where's Beth and her daughter?"

"Inquiring minds want to know."

"Still playing games?"

Frank laughed and then turned abruptly to ice. "People die in my games." He paused. "Hell, call me softhearted, but I'm gonna give you a second chance."

I said nothing.

"You know the American Hotel over on Broadway?"

"What about it?" I finally answered.

"Gather up your supplies. Wait for me there. We'll make a trade. You give me your supplies, I'll give you Beth."

"What about Ashley?" I asked.

"Don't get clever," he warned. "The kid is an insurance policy. After you deliver the goods, I'll radio you where to find her. Don't bring any weapons. If you do, the deal is off."

I laughed out loud. "You really think I believe you? The minute I'm in the street, you'll gun me down."

"You underestimate me. If I wanted you dead, you'd be buried."

I couldn't deny that.

A few years ago a guy from town named Bruno Martz shoved a litter of kittens in a garbage bag. Walking down to the east bridge, one by one and whistling like a mailman, he flung them into the Lehigh River. Afterwards he grabbed a cold one at Pecker's Bar and bragged about drowning the little bastards, as he termed it, in the canal.

Frank had those same narcissistic traits. No matter how far he reached, he couldn't grasp the concept of compassion. In fact, he viewed it as human frailty. In his mind, it was easier to control the world around him by aggressive means as opposed to getting bogged down in the pitfalls of love and kindheartedness. It's the kind of stuff killers are made of.

At the same time and more than once, Frank had the opportunity to kill me. But not even that interested him. At least in my case, he favored the amusement of suffering as opposed to disposal and termination.

"If you're worried about me killing you, walk away," Frank said. "Hunker down in the cellar. Sooner or later help will arrive, but it won't go that easy for the kid or her mother," he assured me. "I know. You think I'm a real hard ass. Maybe that's true. I got no problem with wrapping a wire around both their throats until their faces turn blue. If you decide to walk away, you should think about that Eddie. You're the one that'll have to live with the consequences."

"How do I even know Beth is alive?"

"Always the skeptic," said Frank.

Listening close, again I heard chimes in the backdrop. Still I couldn't place where I heard them before.

"Eddie?" A fraught voice suddenly came over the radio.

"Beth, is that you?" My heart wrapped on my chest. "Where are you? Where's Ashley?"

"Frank has us." Her voice shivered. "He has us and said that he's going to..."

A loud noise, a slap followed by a moan, interrupted the dialogue.

"Enough talk," said Frank. "Be reasonable Eddie. I don't want to hurt anyone, but you got to understand, this is business. Meet me at the hotel. Beth's fate is in your hands," he said, and then everything went silent.

Frank couldn't be trusted. If I went to the hotel, he'd sit in a window ledge or hide behind a hedge. When I got close enough, BAM! I'd take one to the head.

I stared blankly at the radio and bit at my fingernails. That's the trouble with guilt; it ignores sound judgment. He'd murder Beth if I didn't comply with his demands. Ashley would share a similar fate. In a world gone vicious, her chance of survival had about the same odds as falling into a lion pit ten minutes before the noon feeding. Any form of continued existence would be in doubt.

"You gonna push the envelope?" The little guy in my head was back again. *"Get it straight. You can't save them. They're already dead. You'll be next if you try."*

It was sound advice. I needed to cut my losses. Stay hidden until help arrived. Maybe even get out of town. I could hole up in some remote location, at least until the authorities got things back up and running.

Yeah, right.

Blowing cold air through my nostrils, I trudged upstairs and grabbed an empty duffle bag from a closet. In the bedroom underneath some loose floorboards, I had canned vegetables, candy bars, even a box of Captain Crunch cereal. I also had MRE's from the army surplus store. They tasted bad, like dry crackers and spam, but supplied enough nourishment to keep me up and running, at least until I decided to give them all to Frank.

"What the hell?" The voice in my head sounded amazed. *"You're really going through with this? Listen to reason. You can't go trudging off on a suicide mission. The boogeyman is waiting. He'll bury you in the same dark hole as Beth and Ashley. Leave it go. Cut your losses and move on."*

The little guy in my head had a way with words, and of course, he was right. If I stayed low on the radar, things might eventually even out. The authorities would arrive and search for survivors. They might even open a bread and cheese line.

"I'm telling you, you're barreling towards the edge of a cliff," said the pleading voice in my head. *"Last chance, give it up."*

Stuffing the duffle bag with food, I threw it over my shoulder and headed out the door towards the American Hotel.

28

Mr. Hollywood

A faint glimmer of sunlight rose over the eastern mountains. It was morning. Without the cover of darkness, I'd need to be careful. Undesirables were everywhere.

Heading down Fargo Street, I passed the Packer Mansion, a manor once owned by a rich tycoon who made his fortune in the coal industry. The place was a historic landmark, but these days, the windows were smashed and beer bottles littered the ground outside the entrance of the property.

Further down the hill, I rounded the bend at the intersection by Molly's Bar. Just up the street sat the American Hotel. There were no signs of Frank. He could have been hiding behind a curtain in any tenement window or even in Nelly's Pastry Shop across the road. I could almost feel his breath on my neck.

"Enjoying the scenery?" Frank broke in on the radio.

"Let's get this over with," I answered.

"You bring the supplies?"

I held the duffle bag up in the air, certain that he had me under surveillance from an undisclosed location. "Now where's the girl?"

"What girl?" Frank taunted.

"Stop playing games. You said if I brought food, you'd give her to me."

"I'll get to that one," said Frank. "Right now we got other things to contend with. Take a look up the street, over by the traffic light. We got company."

Turning around, I saw a young man, late teens, standing near the crosswalk. Tall and thin with messy brown hair, he stared at me through big green Elton John glasses and sported a long red overcoat with a torn collar. His pants, too short and riding up his ankles, displayed a pair of mismatched tube socks.

"Talk about a geek." Frank whistled. "Check out the threads and goggles. This dude should be living on Sunset Boulevard. I'm telling you, he's Mr. Hollywood. I'm surprised someone didn't shoot him already for using up too much air. Get rid of him."

Mr. Hollywood stepped off the curb. A knife trembled in his hand. He pointed at the duffle bag, clearly favoring a wound on his arm. "What's in the sack?" he asked, trying to sound tough.

"Nothing," I said.

Mr. Hollywood's eyes darted around nervously. "I need food."

"We all do," I reminded.

"Don't make me use this." Shivering in his shoes, he held the knife up and nearly dropped it in the gutter. I don't know what the guy had in mind. I was an unemployed car salesman, about as rough as a wet sponge in a bucket of soap, and he didn't even scare me.

"The kid is grating on me," Frank said over the radio. "Send him packing."

"This is the last place you want to be right now," I told him. "Beat it."

Mr. Hollywood rocked back and forth on his heels. Lowering the knife, his pouty lips hung down over an uneven set of choppers. "I just need a little food, that's all." For a minute I swore he'd start crying.

"I don't have anything to spare." I glanced at the duffle bag.

"Don't even think about giving him any of my supplies," Frank interjected. "You got about three seconds to get rid of that punk. If you don't, I will."

I looked at Mr. Hollywood. The kid appeared beaten down. I had him figured for someone who probably worked the takeout window at McDonalds and spent Saturday nights at the Drive-In with his girlfriend, but now? Skinny as a rail from lack of food, he looked frightened, alone, and struggling for survival.

"Listen," I said sternly. "You got to get out of here. Look around. Check houses, garbage cans, do whatever you have to do to stay alive. Help can't be far off."

Wiping his nose, he tossed the knife on the ground. I couldn't help thinking of a homeless mutt. His sad eyes were lost and caught up in the brutality of the world.

"That's a bad scrape." I pointed at his arm. Yellowish pus oozed from the wound. "I think it's infected. How long did you have that?"

Mr. Hollywood shrugged his head sheepishly.

"Here." I finally slipped a hand in my pocket and pulled out the amoxicillin that Jimmy Stokes gave me. "Take this. It should help."

"Freeze cowboy," Frank sounded off.

"Relax." I held the bottle of antibiotics up in the air. "It's medicine. I got more in the duffle bag if you need it."

"I don't need it," said Frank. "I raided Ned's Pharmacy before all the junkies crashed the place. Hell, I got everything from penicillin to pimple cream, but I'll be damned if I'm wasting any plunder on Mr. Hollywood. Put the meds in the bag with the rest of the stuff."

"He's just a kid Frank," I said loudly. "What, eighteen years old? His arm is infected. If he doesn't get treatment it'll get worse."

"You think I give a rat's ass what he needs?" Frank asked. "Hey Mr. Hollywood, you listening to me boy?" he asked over the radio.

The young man shivered in the cold and pawed at his contaminated arm.

"I said are you listening?" A bullet plunked in a mailbox beside him.

Mr. Hollywood jumped two feet. Scrunching up against the side of a Volkswagen he wrapped his flailing arms around his head.

"There now," Frank said. "That got your attention, didn't it? I think you're trying to screw with me boy. Is that it, you're screwing with me?"

Mr. Hollywood trembled. His eyes moved from window to window, not knowing where the sniper lurked.

"You ignoring me? I asked you a question!"

I couldn't see Frank's face but could almost feel his eyes narrowing with contempt.

"No, no sir," the kid stuttered and looked around in confusion. "Who, who is this?"

Another shot rang out and recoiled off the sidewalk, shattering the window of the Dimmick Library. "Who told you to talk?" The clear sound of a gun's hammer being drawn back again sounded in the radio. "You know what I think Mr. Hollywood? I think you were gonna steal my supplies. You know what happens to someone in North Korea if they get caught stealing?"

"I, I don't know." The kid's pleading eyes shifted towards me.

"People eat the bullet when they steal in those shitty little third world countries," Frank told the kid. "Is that what you want, to eat the bullet?"

The kid sniffled but said nothing.

"Answer me Mr. Hollywood. You answer me now or I swear to God I'll blow a hole the size of a baseball in your head."

"No."

"No what?"

"I, I just want to go home," he whimpered.

Little did the kid know, but this place, this disaster, this human travesty of injustice, had now become home. Forget college and summer vacations at the shore. Class was now in session for a new kind of world, one that hinged on killing thy neighbor for the sake of stale bread.

"I'm gonna give it to you straight Mr. Hollywood. You stepped on my turf," said Frank. "I don't like that. I don't like it at all."

The kid's lips twisted in fear but no words came out.

"What's your take on this Eddie?" Frank summoned me. "Should I kill him?"

"That's enough Frank," I said angrily.

"I'll tell you what," he said smartly. "I promised to give you a chance to save Beth, and by God, I'm gonna give you that opportunity. So tell me cowboy. Someone got to die here, right?" asked Frank. "Should I end Mr. Hollywood's miserable existence or do I put a bullet in Beth's head. You make the call."

"You're crazy," I told him.

"I'd hurry if I were you," he said. "Time is running out."

"Frank, don't do this," I implored him. "You want to shoot somebody?" I yelled. "Then shoot me."

Frank laughed, "Nice comeback but you're not getting off that easy. Hey Mr. Hollywood, are you still with me out there?" He redirected the conversation. "It looks like we got ourselves a hung jury. That leaves me as the judge on this one.

CRUDE

I'm thinking that maybe you deserve to die, right? Go ahead and say it," he ordered. "Tell me you deserve to die."

"I, I can't." The kid's teeth chattered.

"Sure you can. It's a snap," Frank told him. "Just say the words."

The kid's face cracked and tears ran down his cheeks. "I can't."

"You want a bullet in your skull? Say it. Two seconds."

"I..."

"I what?" Frank urged.

"I de, de-deserve..."

"Good dog," Frank taunted. "What do you deserve Mr. Hollywood?"

"To, to, to..."

"To what?" Frank prodded. "Say it asshole. Say it now."

"D, D, D..."

"Say it!"

"Die," the word finally rolled off his tongue.

The sudden sound of another shot echoed in the streets. This one grazed the kid's arm and literally tore fabric off his coat. Yelping, he hit the dirt and covered up.

"Scared you, didn't I?" Frank chuckled. "Maybe next time you'll learn some manners. Now get up and beat it."

The kid got off the ground, started left, went right, then back again, moving without direction like a headless chicken.

"One more thing Mr. Hollywood," Frank said over the radio.

The kid turned but was abruptly interrupted by a well placed bullet to the head. The chunk of lead impacted with the velocity and fierceness of a lightning strike. Mr. Hollywood was dead on arrival before he ever hit the ground.

"Frank!" I threw the duffle bag down. "You killed him!"

"You're too sensitive." Frank snickered. "You really think a kid like that could survive in the world? If anything I alleviated his misery."

"I get it. You're a model citizen," I said angrily.

"You don't sound convinced," said Frank. "You probably think I'm coldhearted. Nothing could be farther from the truth. When I was a kid my old man was never around. His favorite pastime included cheap bourbon and local strip clubs. He staggered home at night and beat me with a belt buckle. What chance did I have in life?"

I listened impatiently. What the hell was this, a confessional? I wasn't a priest. Furthermore, hate, impenetrable as dense fog, glazed my vision. Any sense of compassion once harbored had been washed away, lost at sea. I wanted Frank to die.

"Fucking people like you." Frank droned on, his voice thick and guttural. "In the military I was special ops. I fought for guys like you in Afghanistan, and this is the thanks I get?" he said resentfully. "That kid in the street? He's just another casualty of war. I got no more remorse about gunning him down than dissecting a worm in biology class. War has a way of drumming those things in your head. So does prison. Okay," he admitted. "So I got issues."

The only issue that this bastard had was that someone didn't drive a sword down his throat.

"You think you're the only person who had some tough breaks Frank?"

"Don't get me wrong. I'm not complaining," he said. "It's what made me what I am. Unlike a certain chicken shit car salesman, I got guts."

"You also got the stuff that makes serial killers," I reminded. "Enough talk about the family history. What's the plan Frank? Are you gonna gun me down in the street like you did the kid?" I glanced over at Mr. Hollywood.

"It's like I told you," Frank answered. "You wanted to be a leading actor. I'm gonna give you the chance to put on the red cape. You see that broken window on the second floor of the hotel, right in the middle of the terrace?"

I looked up at the shattered windowpane. "What about it?"

"That's room 216. Beth is in there. Drop the duffle bag and come up."

It was a trap, of course. I'd open the room's door and Frank would be waiting with a smug grin and a loaded rifle.

On the other hand, he could have already shot me in the street. Still something told me that wouldn't satisfy him. He wanted me to crawl on my belly like a snake and then crush me under the heel of his shoe.

"How do I know you won't kill me?" I asked.

"You don't," Frank answered smartly. "Still if I were you, I'd hurry. Any second now, I could fire off a round or slit the girl's throat and deliver her corpse on your doorstep. If you can live with that cowboy, then get on your horse and ride into the sunset. Otherwise, I'd hurry. She has very little time left."

Biting down hard on my lip, I said in the radio, "I'm on my way up."

29

The American Hotel

The front door of the American Hotel stood partly open. Walking in, I shined my flashlight around the lobby. A huge chandelier had been decorated in Victorian décor. Beaded lampshades and cast iron lanterns sat on antique wooden tables. A large mirror hung on the wall beside colorful paintings depicting the artistic mysteries of Italy. Adjacent the check-in desk, windows were festooned in lush satin curtains, and an old-fashioned red fainting couch sat catty cornered in the room. A breakfast table with fossilized donuts on a tray fermented in the cold.

A side door adjacent the lobby led to the hotel cocktail lounge and a dining room. Tables were decorated with wilted roses, dirty dishes and personalized napkins for Mr. and Mrs. Douglas Stacks. A banner, halfway fallen, had been tacked up on an archway that read *Happy 50th and many many More.*

Moving on down the corridor, an unplugged vacuum cleaner and a laundry cart with dirty linen sat in the hall in front of a guest room. Further on, the gruesome scene of an elevator with a leg sticking out of it blocked the door from closing. Gasping, I pulled back against the wall.

"Get a grip," the voice in my head said. *"He's trying to get inside your head. If you let him, you'll be the guy at the elevator's next stop."*

Turning the corner, I walked towards a staircase that led to the second floor of the hotel. The glass on a snack machine at the end of the hall had been kicked in; no doubt poachers looking for a sugar rush.

"How do you like the accommodations?" Frank's gritty voice sounded off in the radio. "Man, the place looks haunted, doesn't it? You'd swear Jack Nicholson was gonna jump out with an axe." He paused. "You still with me cowboy?"

"Just looking for the pool," I answered.

"That's the spirit!" Frank laughed in a creepy voice that made my skin simmer. "You're almost there," he said. "It's kind of scary, isn't it? Listen to the quiet. Nobody is alive in here. Back in the military, we raided houses in Afghanistan and flushed out terrorists. You never knew what you'd find behind closed doors. Sometimes the damn places were booby trapped. I had a friend named Raker Biggs who got blown up in the kitchen of a fast food diner. When the blast went off, he splattered off four walls."

"A shame it wasn't you," I said and kept walking.

Opening the door to a fire exit, I walked up a flight of steps that led to the second floor. Room 216 was only a few doors down the hall. If Frank was waiting for me, so far he showed no signs of it. I considered the idea that he might not be in the hotel. He might have lured me into the place as a distraction, grabbed the duffle bag filled with food and then made a quick escape. I doubted it though. He wasn't the type to go away in a whisper but rather a clap of thunder.

Looking around, a small fire extinguisher hung on a hook against the wall. Sure as hell the element of surprise was gone, but I had no intention of going down without a fight. If I couldn't win the battle I'd put an irreparable dent in Frank's skull. Removing the extinguisher from its mount, I held it in front of me like an iron shield.

Taking a few more steps, I stopped and stared at the closed door of room 216.

"You must be close," Frank said. "I can practically hear you breathe. Are you ready to look fate in the eye?"

"Instead of hiding in some dark hole and waiting to ambush me, why don't you show yourself? I'm not surprised. I always had you pegged as a coward," I taunted.

"Keep talking hero." Undertones of anger swam in his words. "Before this is done, I'll show you who the coward is."

Standing there, the voice in my head knocked again. *What are you waiting for? You got no time to hesitate, let alone breathe. He thinks you'll fold under the pressure. Hike the ball and bust the door down.*

Using my shoulder like a battering ram and without hesitation, I barreled forward and hit the door hard. It flew open and I stormed inside, the fire extinguisher held high overhead.

Turning from side to side, there was no sign of Frank, but shackled to a post and gagged with a strip of torn up bed linen, Beth's haunted eyes stared at me. Something had been tied around her waist; its green glow blinked in the darkness and made a steady blipping noise.

Blip. Blip. Blip.

"Figure it out yet cowboy?" Frank said over the radio and paused. "Yep, it's a bomb."

30

Behind closed Doors

There are moments you prepare for in life, like graduating college, getting married, or maybe that dream vacation to a far off tropical island in the South Pacific. Other moments, not so much.

When I stepped through the door of room 216, I became a victim of unforeseen circumstances. The turn of events didn't just knock on the door; it rammed the son of a bitch down.

Beth's face was bruised. Her wrists twisted in handcuffs that were locked around a corner post, and her eyes, once blue with passion but now dark with fear, stared at me from underneath a gag tied around her mouth. A coat resembling a straight jacket hugged her slender body and a small mechanism, throbbing green, had been fastened snugly around her waist.

"Frank, let her go," I demanded over the radio.

"Are you talking to me?"

"You heard me. We had a deal."

"Sorry. I can't do that." He declined. "I got to say, your woman had a rough night. It takes a lot of slaps to make those apple red cheeks. It's safe to say she won't be this year's cover model for Vogue magazine."

"What's your game Frank?" I asked.

"You sure you want to know?"

"Tell me!"

"Remember that stint in the army I told you about?"

"What about it?"

"Take a look at the vest Beth is wearing," he said. "It's lined with C4."

My muscles stiffened. Beth's face expanded in fear.

"If it explodes," said Frank, "well, just say bones make great projectiles."

"You're insane."

"I'm an original," he differed.

I studied the device around Beth's waist. "How do I know that's real?"

"Sure as hell you're gonna find out," Frank assured me. "You don't become a first rate con without making friends in low places. I met a guy named Randall Stinger in jail. He got indicted by the feds on terrorism charges. The crazy bastard wanted to blow up the American Stock Exchange, not to mention a hot dog vendor on West 95th street who gave him food poisoning.

"While I was in the clink," Frank went on, "Stinger told me he had explosives hidden in a barn outside of Gloucester. He even drew a map. When I got loose, I investigated the claim. It turns out he was telling the truth. Semtex, dynamite, C4, you name it. I packed some up in a knapsack. Of course none of that matters much right now," he reminded. "What does matter is the blinking green widget attached to Beth."

I studied the device. For all I knew the gadget was little more than a battery operated remote control from an RC helicopter that kids fly around houses. Then again, criminals had connections. It was possible that some scumbag in jail had conspiracy issues and concealed explosives. Either way, the mechanism was locked tight around Beth's waist and had no clear way of detachment.

"You got what you want Frank. Let her go. The supplies are outside in a duffle bag."

"I'll get to that," he said. "Right now you got bigger problems. Your girlfriend is in serious danger of imploding. There's still time for you to do something about it."

"What are you talking about?"

"Take a close look," said Frank. "You see those two wires sticking out of the detonator?"

A red and blue one was wedged in the side of the device that was tied to Beth's waist. "What about them?"

"One of those wires detonates the bomb. The other disarms it. All you have to do is figure out which one. There's a wire cutter in the drawer of the vanity. Cut one of them. If things go right, you and Beth can walk out of here and live happily ever after. If things go wrong, well," he paused, "you'll be picking up her pieces in a gutter, all the way down on 4th street.

I stood there immobilized. Frank had all the warmth of an iceberg. He didn't kill for survival; he murdered for amusement. When someone opened the cage door to his cell, they left a lion loose in downtown San Francisco. Sooner than later, someone would get mauled.

"This doesn't need to happen," I told him. "Take the food. We go our separate ways. Nobody has to know anything."

"Who cares if anyone knows?" Frank snapped back. "You're stalling. Roll the dice cowboy. Cut the wire."

"I won't do it."

"I said cut it."

"Not gonna happen."

"Cut the fucking wire or I'll detonate the bomb right now!" he shouted. "You got ten seconds."

In that impossible moment, the uncertainties of life converged on a single point, defined as the red dot on the scope of a rifle, or in this case, a red and blue wire.

I walked over to the vanity. Just as Frank said, wire cutters were inside the drawer, on top of a bible. Pulling them out, I approached Beth. Her frightened eyes followed my every move. Bending down, I removed the gag tied around her mouth.

"We have to do this," I said.

Beth didn't answer. She didn't have to. Her haunted eyes, sunk in pale skin and burnt with the ashes of fear, stared back at me and did all the talking. Sharp spears of terror creased her forehead, extending down to her trembling lips.

"You still with me cowboy?"

"I'm here Frank."

"Good," he said. "I'd hate to think I missed the magic moment. Now cut one of the wires."

My fingers trembled. I moved the cutters from one color to the next. Finally my hand came to rest next to the red one. I looked up at Beth and swallowed hard.

"Do it." She bit down hard on her lip.

I squeezed the handle of the cutters but in the last second, the one that determines the fate of the world, switched to the blue wire and snipped it.

Closing my eyes, I waited for the blast.

Nothing happened after a minute. Not one damn thing. My smile sparkled like the sea when first lighted with rays of morning sunlight and then just as quickly I caught sight of the coming storm.

Digital numbers lit up on the device attached to Beth's waist, five minutes worth of digital numbers. They were counting backwards.

"You never were lucky, were you?" said Frank. "That's a damn shame. I'll give you two a few minutes alone." He paused. "Five of them to be exact."

The radio clicked off.

31

5 ticks of the Heart

Back in college, in those days when I swore I'd conquer the world, I took a summer job in the Wildwoods, a beach town on the coast in Jersey. Eating cotton candy for lunch and swimming in the ocean after work sounded like the perfect itinerary for a college brat. I landed a job at a seaside restaurant called The Blue Caboose. It only paid minimum wage plus tips. I split expenses with four other students in a grungy seaside apartment and slept on a half deflated air mattress on the floor. We were young, dirt poor, and always twitching on the trigger of this thing called life. Those were the best days I ever had.

Along with the locals, students from abroad were bused in to work in the seaside junk shops. They came from everywhere to experience American culture and earn money to pay tuition bills. Enter Tina Carr, an Irish lass with big green eyes who dished up Kohr's ice cream at a stand on the boardwalk and ran the Tilt-a-Whirl down at Morey's Pier.

One day after my shift at The Blue Caboose, I meandered down around the waterfront. The ocean shimmered with all the brilliance of diamonds in the sunlight and seagulls circled the boardwalk waiting for vacationers to throw them pizza scraps. A young Irish girl sat down beside me on a bench. Glancing over, she offered a warm smile and tied her sneakers.

"Tina Carr," she said and nodded, her green eyes twinkling.

I'm telling you straight up; kids fall in love every day. I was no exception. Call it the summer of romantic dreams. The minute I laid eyes on her, BAM! The entire planet shrunk down to a little corner of the world, just big enough for the two of us.

You know what I'm talking about, right? Your heart races like a revved engine. You get this permanent grin dancing on your lips. You're amazed at how beautiful life is with that special person and still scared to death that you might lose them one day. There's something about being young and in love. Its magic sealed with a kiss. Looking back, that's how I remember those warm summer nights by the seaside with Tina Carr: pure magic.

In the weeks that followed, if I wasn't pulling a shift at the Blue Caboose, I was spending time with Tina. June crossed over into July, and July melted into August.

One night, the moon flying high over the ocean, we cuddled up on a blanket on the beach. Tina wore a blue halter and a gardenia in her hair. She hugged my chest as we watched the waves dance under the stars.

"The season is almost over." She looked distant and thoughtful. "I'll be going back to Dublin in a few days," she said sadly and paused. "I'm in love with you Eddie, do you understand?" She turned to me. Tears dotted her eyes like little drops of rain. "I'm happier than I've ever been and now I have to board a plane and leave it all behind. We'll never see each other again."

"Don't say that," I told her.

"It's true." She stared blankly into the ocean.

Pulling Tina close, I ran my fingers through her hair. "We'll stay in touch, maybe come back next summer."

I knew I was lying, at least to myself. She knew it too. We'd never come back. She'd board a plane and disappear into the clouds forever. Time would pass. Memories would fade. But every now and again, she'd think back to the boy she met on the boardwalk, the boy she fell in love with as a young college girl, full of life and discovering the world around her.

I cried in her arms that night.

That was a long time ago. What I remember most about those days was the look in Tina's eyes as she boarded the plane. She tried to be strong for my sake all the while her heart shattered. She even forced a smile as she turned her head and wiped a tear from her eye. Just before she got on the plane, she whispered the words, "I love you." Then it happened. Just that quick she was gone.

Looking back, sometimes I can't quite remember the Irish girl's face, but I never forgot that look as she stepped on the plane. Even after the passing years, it hung on my heart like a ball and chain. It was that look that said, "We'll never pass this way again, and our lives together are done way too soon."

In all the time since that summer by the seaside, I never once saw that look of despair again, at least not until I stood in room 216, staring into Beth's eyes.

A dark shadow of dread hung over Beth. She looked stunned; a sleepwalker who wakes up in the middle of the night to discover she's wandered into a minefield.

"We're gonna find a way out of this." Uncertainty trembling in my fingers, I held Beth's face in my hands.

Looking down at the vest around Beth's waist, it would be impossible for her to remove it without first freeing her arms.

Standing up, I grabbed the wooden post that Beth's wrists were shackled around and shook it hard. The thing wouldn't budge.

"We need to find something to use for leverage." I looked around the room. Flinging the closet door open, I pulled everything off the shelf. There were pillows, blankets, even a crumpled up Dodger's baseball cap that someone stuffed down behind a combination safe. Still there was nothing that would help loosen Beth's restraints.

Glancing at the timer attached to her waist, time ticked away like heartbeats.

4 minutes

I picked up the fire extinguisher and bounced it in my hands. "This has some weight. I might be able to break the chain. Don't move."

Beth pulled the handcuffs tight around the post and closed her eyes.

"Ready?"

"Do it." She held her breath.

In a quick chopping blow, I slammed it against the chain. Still the restraints showed no sign of fracture.

"Damn-it!" I threw the extinguisher across the room, knocking over a table lamp.

I looked at Beth. Hope faded like fleeting clouds on the edge of a storm, all the while the mechanism attached to her waist marked time in one second increments.

"Tick, Tick, Tick," said the timer.

3 minutes

"We're not giving up." I rooted through a drawer in the vanity.

"Eddie," said Beth, her voice quiet and thoughtful.

I barely heard her speak. Hot coals of desperation burned inside of me. The time for words had passed. The stage was set, the house lights beamed down, and the famous final scene rapidly drew closer. Right now we didn't need a good plan; we needed a miracle.

"Eddie," Beth repeated. "Listen to me."

I went to the broken window and peered into the vacant streets. In a cryptic scene, the roads were iced up, and trashcans, toppled over. A dead traffic light sat in the middle of an intersection and Mr. Hollywood, his lethargic face staring into empty sky, laid in a gutter in front of Antonio's pizzeria.

"Is anyone out there?" I shouted. "We need help!"

Outside of the wind, no answer came. People either left town or hid inside boarded up buildings. Instead of welcoming abodes, houses now served as fortresses against intruders who were once friendly neighbors.

"Please Eddie. You've got to listen."

Finally I turned around and looked at Beth, then lowered my gaze to the digital timer attached to her waist.

Tick. Tick. Tick.

2 minutes and counting

"No!" I shouted angrily.

Rushing over to the post, my fists pounded the wood until my knuckles bled. Still it wouldn't move, not even one thin hair.

"Maybe he's bluffing." I pulled the radio out. "Frank, are you there?"

Empty static hissed, stagnant as slow poison.

"Eddie!" Beth again. Her voice was loud. Insistent.

I turned to look. Gulping down fear, her pale complexion and hollowed cheeks floated in a distant stare of sadness rather than dread.

"Eddie," she said. "It's time to go now."

"What?" My eyes widened.

"Go Eddie. Go before it's too late."

"I can't just go and..."

"Yes you can," she cut me off. "You can't save me." She glanced at the doorway. "You can do this."

I dropped to my knees. Maybe it was guilt, probably love, and almost certainly a little of both, but at that moment I put my head in my hands and began to sob.

"It's my fault Beth," I said. "Frank heard me say your name over the radio. If I wouldn't have done that, none of this would be happening."

"You've got to listen to me Eddie," she said softly, almost in a whisper. "You didn't do this. Frank did. It isn't your fault. You have to leave."

"I can't."

"Yes you can." She nodded. "Be strong. Walk out the door. Don't look back. Go Eddie. Go before it's too late."

My eyes shifted to the timer fastened to Beth's waist.

Tick. Tick. Tick.

1 minute and counting

"No!" I sprang to my feet and rammed my shoulder against the wooden post again. Still nothing moved, not even a crack. Frank did his job well. The post was solid as a slab of cement.

"It's finished Eddie."

"No it isn't," I insisted.

"It's done." She looked on in quiet certainty.

Looking at Beth, for an instant I saw a flash of Tina Carr's face, the green eyed Irish girl that I met in the Wildwoods back in college. It was a look that said, "The dance has ended, the music stopped, and the long kiss goodnight is over."

Tick. Tick. Tick.

40 seconds

"Hurry," Beth said again, a desperate tingle in her voice.

My feet were cemented to the floor. How could I leave her to die? How could I go on in life, the memory of her final moments and the pain embraced on her face, forever haunting my dreams?

"I can't just leave."

"Eddie!" she said loudly. "Don't you understand?" Tears fell like warm pearls down her cheeks. "I need you to save my baby. Please Eddie. I need you to save Ashley. She's all that matters. She's all I have. Please," she cried, "give her a chance to live."

I'm not sure where the strength came from. Maybe it was the undefeatable spirit of love in Beth's eyes, that selfless passion that a mother feels for a child placed in danger, but with one last look, the long kiss goodnight ended.

Turning, I ran out of the room and down the staircase. Hurrying through the lobby, I bolted out the front door of the hotel, tripped on the curb and fell headfirst in the gutter. Digging my fingers into the palms of my hands, enough to draw blood, I braced for impact.

The seconds ticked by but there was still no explosion. I waited. One minute. Three minutes. Five minutes. Still nothing.

Pushing myself up on bruised elbows, I stared at the window of room 216. Hope glimmered on my face, brighter than the morning sun lingering behind dark clouds, ready to rise out of the mist. Something went wrong. The bomb didn't detonate.

"Beth!" I shouted. "Hang on. I'm coming back up!"

There was no answer.

"Beth, can you hear me?"

The radio static cleared again. "The savior is on the move again."

"You hear that Frank?" I held the radio in the air. "The bomb didn't go off."

"Don't be so smug. I could gun you down in the street if I want to."

"Like you did the kid?" I looked over at Mr. Hollywood, dead on arrival. "You really want to kill me?" I asked. "Do it." I expected a bullet to cut me square in the eyes or at least take out a kneecap and cripple me from any hope of escape.

"Don't push me," he warned.

Suddenly another voice, barely audible, could be heard in the background of the radio.

"Bravo one. Is anyone on this frequency, anyone at all?"

My eyes brightened. "Hello? Who is this?" I shouted in the receiver. "I need help!"

"This is Sergeant Mills. I'm with the army. What's your position?" His voice started to break up.

"I'm in Thorpe, north of Allentown. Are you coming?"

Sergeant Mills answered, "We're making rounds. Sit tight. Our ETA is..." the transmission trailed off into static.

I looked up at the tall buildings, certain that Frank was holed up in one of them, pointing his gun. "You hear that?" I shouted in the streets. "The army is on their way."

"You really think that's gonna stop me cowboy?" Frank shot back. "Let them come. Who cares?"

"You should care," I yelled. "They're coming Frank. They're coming and they're gonna string you up on a tree with a wire and you know what? I'm gonna grin watching you suffer, you sorry son of a bitch. So what are you gonna do hotshot?" I got up and opened the door of the American Hotel. "You gonna run and hide?" I laughed. "I guess it's true. You're nothing but a coward."

Frank took pause. "You guessed wrong," he said, and the building exploded.

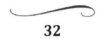

32

The Fire Inside

The exterior wall surrounding room 216 of the American Hotel burst outward in a fiery flash, leaving a hole the size of a pickup truck. The blast was so complete it shattered the storefront window of Leonardo's Ice Cream shop across the street. Even Mr. Hollywood's remains got jolted two inches off the macadam.

Debris struck me on the back of the neck and I was thrown into the street. Hitting the ground, my head bounced off the road.

"Beth!" I groggily shouted.

My eyes widened in horror as the entire second floor of the hotel creaked and then collapsed inward, effortlessly as a sandcastle struck by a rogue wave.

Turning my head, someone stepped out of the shadows near the rear of the hotel, his dark figure filtered in falling dust and debris. Toting a rifle and a duffle bag, Frank marched towards me.

"I don't see any Stealth fighters." Frank looked up in the sky. "It looks like the army stopped off for coffee and donuts."

"You killed her!" Panic washed in my voice.

Removing the strap of the duffle bag from his shoulder, Frank tossed it on the ground. "I told you not to screw with me cowboy." He positioned the rifle underneath my chin. "Right about now? My guess is that you could pick up pieces of your girlfriend all the way down in Mexico."

I stared back, refusing to blink. "You're gonna pay for this."

Frank shifted his gaze from house to house. "Take a look around. People are hiding in kitchens and basements. Most of them see us. They know you got a gun pointed at your head. But are they going to help you?" He shook his head doubtfully. "You're all alone out here, and those people? They're sheep lined up for a slaughter, too frightened to do anything. That's the difference between me and them." He turned and spit. "People like me flourish in desperate times. In fact, we rule it."

"Why the sermon Frank? If you want to pull the trigger, then do it." I practically dared him.

After a minute, "I don't think so." Lighting a cigarette, he blew a smoke in the frigid air. "Shooting you would be too easy." He glanced at Mr. Hollywood fermenting on the sidewalk. "People got killed out here today. That's on your head. Maybe you should sleep on that for awhile." Picking up the duffle bag, he threw the strap over his shoulder. "Sweet dreams cowboy."

Grinning like the devil, Frank gave me a kick to the side of the head with the heel of his boot just before everything turned dark.

I'm not sure how long I lay there. Hypothermia didn't set in so I suspect minutes as opposed to hours.

Upon waking, the first thing I saw was the American Hotel where Beth had been held captive. The second floor was missing, and the first, littered with debris. Broken bricks from the exterior of the building were thrown on to the sidewalks and awnings of neighboring buildings. There was even an ironing board catapulted into the middle of the intersection.

Disoriented, I stood up on shaky legs and stumbled towards the hotel.

"Beth!" I shouted in the entrance door, blown off its hinges. One look told me that nobody could survive the blast. Everything from the front desk to a chandelier in the lobby had been reduced to rubble. Quick as a snip of a wire, Beth was gone.

Turning my head, I looked suspiciously at the windows of surrounding houses. Frank might have me scoped but I doubted it. He wanted the last images of Beth's terrified face, moments before she died, etched in my mind. The point was to make me suffer for awhile before he killed me.

With one last look, I turned away and walked down the street.

I couldn't help but to feel as if something died in me, almost as if someone took a pocket knife and sliced away the core of my emotions. A dazed look and an incredulous stare played in my eyes. Maybe I was in shock. I didn't feel anger or remorse. I didn't feel anything. In a way, that scared the hell out of me. In the end, lack of empathy is the perfect genetic code for a killer, and as far as I could tell, I was well on my way to walking that dark and nameless road.

Further down the street, two men dressed in ragged clothes leaned against the side of the courthouse. One of them hummed an old Buddy Holly song and rubbed his hands together to keep warm. They were drinking something; maybe a bottle of wine. Both men iced up when I passed by on the opposite side of the street. I didn't know who they were. I didn't want to know. A few weeks back those guys could have been digging ditches or selling magazine subscriptions for Publisher's Clearing House, but today? People killed for stale bread.

I moved along quickly and out of sight.

"You copying me?" My radio crackled with static again. "This is Serg... Mills, Unit... States Army."

I pulled the receiver out of my pocket. "Mills, you there?"

"You're breaking up. I can hardly hear you."

"Mills!" I shouted. "Where are you? What's your ETA?"

"Can't answer that. We're near Allentown, headed north but the roads are impassable. Abandoned cars are everywhere. You still there?"

"I'm here."

"Listen up," said Mills. "Choppers are gonna airlift food and supplies. What's your position?"

"Thorpe."

"Say again?"

"Thorpe!" I repeated louder.

"Pass the word," Mills answered. "We're using high school football fields as landing pads and staging areas. Warn everyone not to storm the supply line. Martial law is in effect. We got orders to shoot if anyone doesn't comply."

"Mills, how long until you get here?" The radio filled with static. I tapped it against my hand. "Mills, are you still there?"

The transmission went dead again.

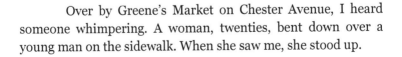

Over by Greene's Market on Chester Avenue, I heard someone whimpering. A woman, twenties, bent down over a young man on the sidewalk. When she saw me, she stood up.

"Can you help me?" She wiped a sleeve over her damp eyes.

I kept walking.

"Please mister." Her downturned lips shivered in the cold. "It's my boyfriend. He's hurt real bad."

As I walked, I remembered a few years ago driving to Pittsburgh to see a Steelers game. Just outside the parking lot I saw a man in tattered clothes hugging the corner of a tenement building and warding off the cold. He held a tin cup with fingerless mittens and a sign that read, *I am homeless*. Tailgate parties were in full swing. Steaks sizzled on grills. People drank beer and whooped it up, all the while passing him by on the street as if he were a dirty little secret that nobody wanted to talk about. I tossed five dollars in his tin cup, but looking back at the indecency of the world, I can't help but to think that in the end, maybe we all got what we deserved.

Halting my pace, I turned to look at the young woman. She wore layered coats, grey sweatpants and mismatched shoes. Sprawled out on the ground, her friend had a bloodied nose and lip.

"What happened?" I asked.

"I don't know." Lowering herself and sitting Indian-style on the ground, she cradled her boyfriend's head in her hands. "Someone came by. Jake asked him if he had any food or water to spare." Holding his gut, her friend coughed and she ran her fingers through his hair. "He came over, smiled, and started hitting Jake for no reason, over and over." She cried harder. "He was carrying a gun and a big sack."

"A sack?"

"Yes."

"Like a duffle bag?"

"Yes, but..."

"Who was with him?" I cut her off. "Was there a little girl?"

"He was alone," she said, still stroking her boyfriend's forehead. "He just started hitting him. He looked crazy."

Frank again, spreading his cheer around the streets.

"Which way did he go?" I asked.

The girl pointed up Broadway.

Walking over, I bent down. Frank really did a number on the guy. His nose was broke and he had more than one bad laceration around the mouth, no doubt compliments of a steel-tipped boot. He also had a considerable gash on his left arm, probably from broken glass littering the ground.

Reaching in my pocket, I pulled out a rolled up tourniquet that I kept on hand for emergencies. "This'll help stop the bleeding." I wrapped it around his arm.

The girl shivered, not so much from the cold as the fear of losing her boyfriend.

"What's your name?" I asked.

"Marcia," she said, twisting the ends of her lank and unwashed hair.

"Okay Marcia," I said calmly. "This is what you're gonna do. Take your boyfriend, Jake is it?"

She nodded.

"Take Jake across the bridge." I pointed. "Walk to the top of Center Street. Use the alleys and backstreets where people won't see you. Then go to the high school football field. You know where that is?"

Shaking, Marcia stared at me.

"Do you know where that is?" I asked again.

"Yeah... yes," she stammered.

"An army helicopter is gonna land there. They'll help you, understand?" I stood up and began walking away.

The girl shouted, "Please mister. Are you just going to leave us here?"

I kept walking. My mind was a blank slate. You might say I was in the zone, at least that's what my old football coach used to say.

"Don't be a wimp Slate. Get in the zone," he'd bark at me, slapping me on the helmet. *"That's your world out there. Nothing else exists."*

That's where I was. Helicopters and rescue didn't matter. The only thing I could see was Beth's desperate eyes pleading for the life of her daughter. Somewhere within me, a fire burned, unquenchable and thirsty for blood: Frank's blood.

"Please," the young woman begged. "I don't think we can make it alone. What if he comes back?"

I didn't answer.

"Are you listening?" she shouted, her words rattled in desperation. "Where are you going?"

Finally I turned and looked into her teary face. "I'm gonna kill the son of a bitch."

33

Whatever happened to Saturday Night?

I'm not sure how long I walked but my feet were blocks of ice. Yawning with exhaustion, I stumbled against porch railings. Once I even fell in a drainage ditch.

"Save her Eddie." Beth's shadowy voice echoed. *"Save Ashley."*

That presented a problem. Frank could be hiding out in an abandoned house, a pool hall, the local library. Even in a small town, if someone didn't want to be found, options were unlimited.

I stumbled along down a path by the railroad tracks, towards Shade Avenue. Again a sensation of being watched settled in on me. Several times I thought I heard footsteps trailing behind, but when I turned around, nobody was there.

One thing was certain; I couldn't continue much further without rest. Across the street sat Hardy's Auto Shop, the building's shingles flapping in the cold wind. The window on the front door had been smashed. Reaching in, I unlatched the lock and stepped inside. A Ford Focus with bald tires and a crinkled up bumper sticker of a peace sign sat on a lift. Old newspapers and a Playboy magazine had been strewn on a dusty desk.

The springs creaked when I sat down on a lumpy red couch in the corner of the garage, perhaps used for customers waiting for their vehicles. Over near the door, for a minute I thought I saw a shadow move.

"Is somebody there?"

The room remained noiseless.

Blowing in my hands, I rubbed them together briskly. A calendar sat on a table stained with what looked like dried coffee or perhaps grease. Picking up the calendar, I counted the days since the oil disaster began.

"Saturday," I whispered and leaned back on the couch.

I forgot it was Saturday. Then again, these days it didn't matter much. Time stopped when the oil bellied up. Still, I used to love Saturday nights. Back when I was a teenager, Beth would jump in this old rusted out Chevy that I cruised around town in. We'd head over to the Opera House, a rundown little playhouse in the historic district where the locals would put on plays.

My attention shifted again when I heard someone bump into a chair or a toolbox.

Jumping off the couch, I reached behind me and pulled a tire iron off a workbench. "Who's there?"

I could just make out two dark figures. One crouched by the doorway and the other bent down alongside a car with the engine in pieces.

"Nobody man." Someone by the door finally stood up.

"What do you want?"

"You got any food, meds, whatever?"

"I'm empty." I tapped my pockets. "Just here to get out of the wind."

Glancing at his cohort, the man by the door took a step forward, switched on a flashlight and shined it in my eyes. "We don't want any trouble," he said. "Just hand over your supplies. Everybody goes away happy." He took another step.

The thug didn't get it. I had no food. Other than what little rations were still hidden in my house, Frank toted the rest away in a duffle bag.

"That's close enough!" I banged the tire iron on the workbench.

The thug lowered the light. Shifting to the left, his partner pivoted around behind me.

I quickly spun around, ready to strike, but it was too late. A hard blow to the back of the neck, perhaps with a hammer or wrench, sent me to the floor. Just before I blacked out, I glanced over at the crinkled calendar that sat atop the work table.

"Saturday night," I mumbled incoherently.

"What?" One of the thugs said in a shadowy voice.

"Shut him down," his partner ordered.

"You mean kill him?"

"I said shut him down," he repeated loudly. "Knock him out." Leaning over, he went through my pockets while the other one, barely out of his teens, stared at me.

The sudden image of Beth flashed across my mind. Back when we were young, that smile of hers lit up the stars every night. Those days were simple and full of life. We'd cruise around on a Saturday night, that unquenchable feeling of love burning in our souls.

Glancing over at the calendar, I mumbled incoherently, "Whatever happened to Saturday night?"

One of the thugs raised an eyebrow. "What did he say?"

"Who cares," the other one answered. "Time to get some shuteye." Raising his foot, he kicked me in the face. Groaning, my thoughts drifted off into a dream.

34

The Hippie Shake

Dressed in a sleeveless tie-dyed tee, a gypsy skirt and Birkenstock sandals, Beth could have been a throwback from the Woodstock era, all the while Joe Cocker flailed on stage in the background.

"I bought this at the thrift shop." She twirled around and modeled her flowered skirt. "You like it?"

I nodded and smiled, not just because she was beautiful, but because youth is such a brilliantly irresponsible age. You only get to go there once; don't waste it.

My hometown held an annual Earth Day festival. Conceived in the crucible of the sixties generation, bands rattled and hummed Grateful Dead tunes in front of coffee shops and town pubs. Ruth's Gem Shop, a standard hippy store that was loaded with love beads and headbands, had a welcome mat at the front door that read, *No Shoes Required*. Patrons garbed in psychedelic shirts, the free spirited counterculture, came from everywhere and burned herbs in the alley beside the place.

Only days before I packed up my hopes and dreams in a suitcase before heading off to college, I attended the festival with Beth. In the town square, vendors with long hair and gold earrings made killer profits from tourists bused in from places like Greenwich Village and New Hope.

"I'll take that one." I pointed at a Boho flower headband and an Indian beaded bracelet.

Beth slipped the bracelet on her wrist and tucked the headband around her hair.

"How do I look?" she asked all the while Brad & Luke, a local musical duo, belted out an old Beach Boys' classic.

"It's beautiful," I told her.

"Really?"

"Trust me. You could be Jerry Garcia's head groupie."

Beth smiled, bent forward and kissed my cheek.

We walked up Main Street and browsed the town's small shops and eateries, including The Big Melt, an ice cream emporium whose claim to fame came in the form of a large chocolate swirl cone topped with peanuts and syrup.

Later that evening we moseyed up the sidewalk towards the Opera House. The place was a small venue playhouse where the locals got an opportunity to get on stage and perform to the public at five bucks a head. Beth had this dream about being a ballerina or an actress. She always loved that kind of stuff.

"Maybe someday I'll be a dancer on Broadway." She whirled around in front of the Opera House.

"I wouldn't be surprised," I told her.

Catching her breath, she walked over to the side of the building and ran her finger down a crevice in the bricks. "Did I ever tell you about the night I got lost in this theater?"

I tilted my head questionably.

"I was just a little girl. It still gives me the chills thinking about it." She shivered. "I ended up in a room, a dark place."

"What do you mean by a dark place?" I put a shielding arm around her.

"That was a long time ago." She laughed, her hair blowing in the warm wind. "Do you hear that?" She changed the subject. "It's a beautiful noise."

She was talking about the wind chimes of course. Dozens of them ornamented the windows of the building. On a breezy night, you could hear them tinkling all the way down on Railroad Street.

"Eddie, can I ask you something?"

I shrugged. "What is it?"

"Do you believe in fate?" She looked at me thoughtfully, her hair tucked under a headband.

I thought about it for a minute. "Why do you ask?"

"My aunt used to tell me that everything happens for a reason. Everywhere we go and everything we do, we're there because we're supposed to be there. Everything means something." A breeze passed by and the wind chimes tinkled.

You really had to love the girl. Beth was a free spirit. She didn't just love life; she danced through it. Still as we stood there in the early evening of a Saturday night, a shadow of sadness, almost as if a cloud passed over the sun, crossed her eyes.

"We'll be leaving for college soon," she said. "Do you think we'll drift? Sometimes people do that. They drift." She paused, her distant gaze staring into the landscape. Taking a deep breath, she looked in my eyes. "Even if we're apart, I think we'll find each other again. That's how fate is," she told me. "It doesn't matter what rivers you go down because they always meet the sea."

I squeezed Beth's hand. "I won't lose you."

"So you really like me?" she asked.

Smiling, my face turned apple red.

"Tell me how much." She turned playful and tickled my ribs. "Go ahead and say it. You love me, don't you, hmmm?"

What the hell kind of a question was that to ask? I was an eighteen year old kid trying to act cool for his girlfriend. The thing is, Beth had a way of stripping down all my defenses.

"You know I'm crazy about you," I said shyly.

"Really?"

"Yes, really."

Beth's face beamed brighter than the sun but then just as quickly wilted like a flower. Twirling around, she splashed the wind chimes festooned on the Opera House with her fingers. The sound chimed all around us and echoed against the houses. Sighing, she finally looked at me sadly and said, "Then why did you let Frank kill me?"

My eyes opened with a start. It was dark. Pitch black.

"Just a nightmare," I whispered and wiped a film of sweat off my face.

At first I didn't know where I was. Then I remembered. I was in Hardy's garage. A couple of goons blindsided me. Shifting around, I tried to move legs but something heavy weighted them down.

"You really piss me off, you know that?" A grumpy voice abruptly came over the radio.

My heart beat faster. Frank again. He wasn't done playing games. I pulled the radio out of my pocket.

"What's wrong Frank, afraid to face me?"

"Don't push the envelope," he warned. "People sometimes get what they wish for."

"You're a loser Frank, a second rate con."

"I said be quiet." Heat rose in his voice.

"If you're such a bad ass, then come and get me," I taunted, trying to draw the shark out of the water.

"If I wanted to kill you, it'd be a snap."

"Is that so?"

"Don't take my word for it. Turn on your flashlight."

"What?"

"Turn it on," he cut me off. "It's sitting on the floor, just to the left of you."

I felt around in the dark and a wave of dread washed over me. The flashlight was exactly where Frank said it would be. Turning it on, my eyes opened wide.

"You getting the message, cowboy?" he asked.

I got it alright. The weight across my legs wasn't something that fell off a shelf. It was one of the men who attacked me. The thug stared blankly at the ceiling. His throat had been slit and peeled open like a ripe orange from ear to ear.

Over by a car in a corner bay, the other man suffered a similar fate, only this one still had the knife sticking in his heart as if it were a stake nailed into a vampire.

Gasping, I rolled the dead body off me and quickly got to my feet.

"Do we understand each other?" Frank sniggered.

"You killed them." I stared at the bodies littering the room.

"Who else?" He sounded as if he earned bragging rights. "Earlier this evening I saw you skulking around. Those two hoods followed you into the garage. Call me crazy, but I guessed they weren't collecting Sunday school dues for the local church."

"You're a murderer."

"I had to protect my investments, right?" Frank reasoned. "Thinking about it, you're pretty goddamn ungrateful. You should be thanking me for saving your miserable hide."

"You're not gonna get away with this."

"That's a laugh." Frank chuckled. "I already did get away with it. Face it," he said. "The world we grew up in is gone. This isn't the American judicial system; I make the laws now."

Frank sounded confident. In control.

Dangerous.

Regardless and despite Frank's chilling voice, my attention was still drawn elsewhere. I heard something in the radio's background. There were pinging noises. Chimes. Dozens of them.

"You still with me hotshot?"

"Right here Frank." I put the receiver against my ear, listening closer to the chimes.

"I decided to give you a second chance. Hey, what are friends for, right?"

"A second chance?"

"That's right. You're coming to work for me Eddie," he said. "Hell that should make you happy. With the entire economy in collapse, I got my pick of applicants but settled on a second rate car salesman." He chuckled and then grew serious. "I need food Eddie. Supplies and guns. You're gonna get them for me."

"What makes you think I'd do anything for you?" I laughed.

"Take a look at the sad souls on the floor," he suggested. "That's Ashley's future staring you in the face if you don't do everything I say. I'll k ill her, do you understand Eddie? It won't be as simple as a gunshot to the heart. I'll put some care into it before she dies. I know," he said. "Some people are real bastards. I'm one of them," he admitted. "But I'm telling you, don't make the kid go through that kind of torment."

"You're a monster." Gripping the radio, my knuckles turned white.

"That's true," Frank concurred. "Still it doesn't change the itinerary. If you don't comply with my demands, Ashley will be dead by this time tomorrow."

Again I heard chimes in the backdrop of the radio. Not just any chimes.

Wind chimes.

"Are you listening to me?" Frank's voice raked with defiance. "Get me what I want. If you don't, there'll be consequences, understand?"

A gust of wind rattled the walls of the garage. Almost simultaneously, the chimes rang out again. Dozens of chimes, the kind that were draped in the windows of the theater at the Opera House.

"Everywhere we go and everything we do, we're there because we're supposed to be there. Everything has a reason," Beth once told me as we stood in front of the Opera House, splashing the wind chimes with her hands.

"You're making me impatient cowboy." Frank's voice grew edgy. "Do we have a deal or not?"

Pausing, I told him, "I'll be seeing you sooner than you think. Much sooner."

I clicked the radio off.

35

Harry Katz

Back in the college days, I had a psychology class that focused on serial killers and the psychopathic mind. We did a case study on a man named Robert Black. Back in the eighties, the guy kidnapped two young girls and held them hostage in his house for three years. There's no telling what kind of tortures they endured. In the end he strangled them with a piece of rope and then dumped the remains in the Trent River. In time the authorities caught him. Black got a life sentence but never got the death penalty. For all I know, when the oil famine hit, he escaped jail and was back out on the streets piling up the body count.

I got to tell you, it really pisses me off. Liberal Rights Activists and the Right to Life Committee didn't get it. Some people just needed to be disposed of.

Frank was one of those people. He even bit off a cashier's ear at a convenience store during a failed robbery attempt. His recent acts of terrorism had steadily risen in the gruesome pools of criminal behavior. When some guard left the cage door to his cell open, the monster came out and quickly became a slave to beastly appetites. The body count rose, and unlike serial killers such as Gacy and Dahmer, Frank showed no signs of guilt, moral sensibility, or even a cooling off period.

Regardless, Frank didn't kill me. My guess is he looked at me as the bad dog that refused to comply with the house rules. Killing me would only serve as an admission of defeat in his struggle for domination. Rather than cut me down with a bullet, by God, he'd beat me into submission.

No matter what the premise, the devil walked in the dark and none of the details favored Ashley's survival. She was spoils of Frank's private war. When he grew tired of her, he'd get rid of her.

"Save her Eddie." Beth's voice whispered in my head. *"Please, save my baby."*

Looking around the garage, my eyes again landed on the dead bodies of the two assailants and the brutality with which they had been disposed of. Time was short.

Taking a deep breath, I headed out the door.

No stars shined and darkness ruled the night with an iron fist. I cut across a woodsy trail beside Sam Miller's baseball field and then towards Hill Road. Houses were sparse in that part of town. The wind moaned in the trees, almost as it were a battle cry of things to come.

At the bottom of Hill Road, Victorian homes lined the main avenue. The once touristy streets bursting with small shops and local pubs had become a haunt for cold and lifeless shadows.

Not far up the street, the Opera House came into view. The place was constructed in the 1800's and featured a Romanesque tower, a small concert hall and balcony seating. The theater held hundreds of acts throughout the years. But it wasn't nostalgia that interested me. It was the wind chimes, dozens of them draped on the windows. The sound filtered down the streets, and moreover, in the radio transmissions sent by Frank.

He was close.

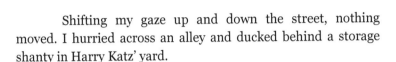

Shifting my gaze up and down the street, nothing moved. I hurried across an alley and ducked behind a storage shanty in Harry Katz' yard.

I met Harry a few times. Small towns are like that. The neighbors know everyone. The big galoot loved entertaining people. He threw parties and was the first person to put a sombrero on his head and dance on a tabletop.

Still, Harry was a military brat. After two tours in Iraq, he became well versed in weaponry. If the guy was holed up in the house, he wouldn't hesitate to fire off a bullet in someone's head.

I crept over to the porch and looked in the window. I didn't see any movement. The backdoor had also been partially kicked in and torn from its hinges. Poachers were abroad and probably scoured the place for food.

"Harry?" I poked my head inside the door. "You here man? It's Eddie Slate."

I shined my flashlight around. The refrigerator door hung open, and the kitchen table, overturned. A melted candle sat on a counter next to a toaster. The house looked vacated. That didn't give me much confidence. Harry could be crouched up with a rifle behind a corner of a couch, ready to unload.

Further on, a music CD of some band called Fantasy sat on a coffee table. Hush puppies were kicked at the foot of an easy chair. An ashtray stuffed with butts was tipped over on the floor. Harry smoked liked a California brush fire and the

Surgeon General would have issued a health citation if he ever walked in the place.

Trembling but determined, I walked over to a flight of steps and climbed to the second floor.

Once upstairs, I turned left in the hall and into the bathroom area. A roll of toothpaste sat on the sink alongside a tipped over bottle of mouthwash. I pulled the shower curtain open and half expected to see Harry staring back at me grasping a semi-automatic, but the only sign of life was a black rat seated on its hind legs, next to a drain.

Moving on, untidy sheets and dirty dungarees scattered the hall. The only clothes kept in pristine shape were an old army uniform that hung in an archway that led to a study.

Inside, books and gun magazines were piled up in boxes and on tabletops. Most of them referenced political turmoil, here and abroad. But I didn't come to discuss JFK conspiracy theories or an assassination coup in the Mid East. I needed a surveillance point. When I saw the French doors with the colored glass, I hit pay dirt.

Peering out the doors, a storage shed sat squarely in the yard of the Opera House, directly beside a rusted fire escape on the second floor of the theater. All entrances and exits to the building were visible. It was just a matter of getting Frank to show his face.

I pulled out the radio. "Frank?"

After a minute, "If it isn't the lone ranger."

"Where's Ashley?"

"What makes you think I didn't kill her?" Amusement danced in his voice.

"What makes you think I won't kill you?" I countered.

Listening close, the wind chimes sang out loud in unison, this time in both the radio's transmission and the outside of the courtyard of the Opera House.

Still there were no signs of Frank. The streets, cryptic and secretive, had danger painted all over them.

For some reason a story my Uncle Leo told me flashed in my mind. He served in the Nam as a tunnel rat. The Viet Cong built underground passages in the jungle to use as storage and training facilities. Armed with a pistol and bayonet, he'd crawl through them, intent on eradicating the underground population. Sometimes the enemy hid inside dark holes with spears. They would jump out and impale the soldiers as they crawled through the subterranean battleground. That's the kind of thing I expected from Frank; every dark corner had a spear, and more likely a hot bullet, targeted at my heart.

"So you're gonna kick my ass?" asked Frank.

"That's the plan," I told him, my eyes glued to the outside of the theater and searching for movement.

"Get serious cowboy." Frank laughed. "You grew up with a golden nipple in your mouth. You're a car salesman, not a bounty hunter. Don't take me on," he warned. "Do yourself a favor. Go find food, supplies, maybe some guns. Bring me the goods. If you're lucky, I'll let Ashley keep breathing," he said. "Otherwise, your stay of execution along with the kid is over. If we meet again, sure as hell I'll cut you to pieces."

Frank sounded tough as truck tires. Still something in his tone sounded desperate.

Years back I read about a plane that went down in the Andes. For two months survivors fed on casualties frozen in the snow. Outside of what I stuffed in a duffle bag, Frank probably hadn't eaten much these days. Once those provisions were

199

exhausted, he wouldn't be eating at all. Just like everyone else, he rode that same flight in the Andes and headed into uncharted territories unless he found more rations.

"Talk is cheap," I told him. "If you're so brave, meet me face to face."

"You're courageous as hell for someone who is about to give up the ghost." Irritation crusted Frank's voice. "Back in the army I had a drill sergeant with an attitude like yours. That ignorant bastard rode me like a mule. One day he made me do pushups for an hour in the rain. Finally I curled up a fist and busted him in the nose so hard that it timbered over on the opposite side of his face."

I stared at the radio, unable to comprehend why Frank insisted on telling me his life history. Maybe he viewed me as a sympathizer. I once read an article where Ted Bundy, convicted serial killer, received scores of love letters from needy women who wanted to nurture him until he expired on an electric chair at Raeford Prison in Florida. But I wasn't a woman and didn't want to nurture Frank; I wanted to crash a 747 on his head.

"You know what the military does when you punch a higher up?" Frank droned on. "The review board gave me a dishonorable discharge. That's right; it ruined my life. Nobody would hire me. Maybe I could have landed some candy ass job like you. Nope," he complained. "That drill sergeant had to get in my way."

Preoccupied with self-pity, Frank continued bellyaching about his bad breaks in life. It'd be the perfect time to catch him off guard and launch an attack. The plan was simple. Draw him into the street, sneak up from behind and kill him. The question was where to find him.

One thing was clear; I needed a weapon.

Opening a desk drawer in Harry's study, I found nothing but a few sticks of stale gum and an unpaid parking ticket. There was even part of a fermented cheese sandwich.

Scanning the rest of the room, I didn't see any firearms. A military brat like Harry would have them but the gun cabinet in the corner of the room had been emptied. Harry either packed the weapons up when he vacated the premises or looters broke into the house and stole them.

"Yep," Frank continued. "You don't know what it is to be the underdog. When I got discharged from the army and couldn't find any work, I swore that I'd find that lousy drill sergeant. I'd make him suffer."

I scoured the drawer and picked up a letter opener but it was hardly a match for a marksman firing a rifle.

"Do you understand me?" asked Frank.

I didn't answer.

"We're adults here. Let's be honest," Frank said. "I don't like you Eddie, and people I don't like? Generally they end up with flies buzzing around their eyes. What do you think cowboy. Are you ready to meet your maker?"

"Says the warrior," I taunted. "You're a coward Frank. Stop hiding. Come and fight."

"Let me explain something hotshot," he said. "The next time I see you? It'll get ugly. You'll get the same treatment I gave that drill sergeant. He screwed with me and found out the hard way."

"You're all wind Frank, no action," I mocked.

A closet sat in the corner of the room. With any luck I'd find a gun or a good solid club inside of it. Walking over, I turned the knob and opened the door.

"That's right cowboy," Frank said smartly. "That drill sergeant I was talking about? His name was Harry Katz."

And that's when it happened. Frank's dirty little secret tumbled out on the floor.

Alongside a pair of muddy sneakers, Harry Katz curled up on the floor, his arms and legs bent in odd directions. A knife was hammered in his throat. Harry's teeth, broken as jagged glass, were knocked cleanly out of his mouth.

"There now," said Frank. "I'm thinking you got the message loud and clear."

I looked frantically around. The bastard knew I was in the house.

"Where are you?" I shouted over the radio.

"If I were any closer, we'd be lovers," he said in a guttural voice.

An instant later, glass sprayed everywhere as Frank crashed through the French doors.

36

The Devil in the Red Fedora

Back in school we had a bully named Charles Railbird. One day Freddie Walker accidentally bumped him in the playground. Railbird shrugged it off, but three days later, retaliated by picking up a desk chair in English class and bashing it over Freddie's skull. The blow sent him to the hospital to get stitches. Railbird showed no more remorse over the incident than a curious kid scrutinizing a frog soaked in formaldehyde.

Railbird got expelled from school. I never saw him again until his picture appeared on the front page of the morning newspaper. After an argument with his wife, he strangled her with a stereo cord and then discarded her body in a dumpster behind a restaurant in Chinatown. Sopping the inside of the dumpster with gasoline, he pulled out a lighter and lit her up. An autopsy later revealed that Railbird's spouse was probably still alive for the campfire.

Later that night the police arrested him at a convenience store buying a pack of cigarettes and a takeout coffee.

"She nagged me about things, like what to eat for dinner," he told the cops from the rear seat of a police cruiser. "Women, huh? She just had to pick a fight."

The policeman glanced in the rearview at Railbird. "So you argued a lot?"

Railbird paused, a smirk on his lips. "Not anymore."

What stuck with me through the years was Railbird's vacant expression and mindless stare. There was something gone in his eyes. It was as if someone carved out a Halloween pumpkin and left nothing inside but an empty shell, devoid of all empathy and warmth. It was that same look of twisted aggression that floated in Frank's face as he crashed through the doors at Harry Katz' house.

"I'm back," he announced.

Carrying a loaded rifle and an attitude, he even wore the red fedora that he found in the upstairs closet of my house.

Glass exploded everywhere. A morbid grin painted across Frank's lips. He jumped in the room and hit the floor running, firing off a quick round from his rifle. The bullet missed and landed in the rear wall.

Whirling around, I picked up a table lamp and flung it. Frank ducked. The fedora flew off his head and the lamp shattered on the floor.

Before Frank could pull the trigger again, I tackled him. Grappling for control of the gun, he swung around and caught me on the side of the head with an elbow. The blow toppled me to the floor. Frank plunked down squarely on my chest. Smiling grimly, he shoved the gun barrel under my chin.

"We meet again cowboy." His black eyes, hollow chasms of detached vengeance, glared at me. For an instant the bleak face of Charles Railbird again flooded my memory. "Sorry to be the bearer of bad news," he said. "Your fifteen minutes of fame are up."

I struggled to move. Frank's weight wouldn't allow it. I was pinned tight to the carpet. A frayed rope of survival quickly slipped from my fingers. I needed something to hang on to.

"Save her Eddie." Beth's voice snapped in my head. *"Please, save Ashley. She's just a little girl."*

"Time to say adios amigo." Frank's finger itched at the trigger. "Just in case you're interested, I still have Ashley, and you know something? I'm gonna teach the brat a lesson, know what I'm talking about Eddie?" He winked. "I'm gonna do things to her and when I'm done? I'm gonna kill her. I'm gonna kill her and leave her bones rotting in some dark alley. Give that some thought while you're gasping for your last breath of air."

"Go to hell." I glared ferociously.

Frank grinned. "You first."

Unless you've met terror face to face, you can't imagine the result that fear can have on someone's physical strength. Adrenaline dumps into the bloodstream. The heart races and delivers a pipeline of energy to muscles. It's the biological equivalent of ramming the pedal to the floor of a Porsche on an open highway. When you're pinned to a carpet and looking down the wrong end of the barrel of a gun, that's the kind of physical desperation that courses through your body.

"Ready to die?" Frank jammed the gun tight against my neck.

In a desperate effort, I pushed hard and toppled Frank off me. Grabbing a wedge of broken glass off the floor, I slashed it in the air. The glass caught him in the chest. Arrogance turned to stunned surprise, long enough for me to knock the gun from his hand. Lunging forward, I grabbed it and quickly got to my feet.

"Don't hesitate," the little voice in my head shouted frantically. *"Pull the damn trigger!"*

Firing a quick round, the bullet went wide right. Frank quickly retreated back to the French doors.

"Don't move!" I shouted.

Frank's face turned into a mass of unmeasured hate. "You want the kid? Pick her up in pieces." Turning, he quickly ran out the door and disappeared into darkness.

"Don't stop," the voice got desperate. *"The kid is in trouble. You started this thing. Finish it."*

Gripping the rifle tight, I trailed after Frank in pursuit.

37

Ghosts in the Darkness

Outside, Harry Katz' terrace sat only a few feet away from a large shed in the courtyard of The Opera House lawn. A dilapidated fire escape with rusty steps, weathered with age, led to an emergency exit on the second floor of the building.

"Hey cowboy," Frank shouted through a busted window from inside of the theater. "You gonna make me wait all day? We got unfinished business."

Eyeing the icy roof, it was a long jump. I glanced down at a sizeable gash on my knee, undoubtedly incurred from a shaving of glass while wrestling with Frank on the floor. The truth is, wounded or not, I was about as athletic as an aged tortoise. If I hoped to make it to the shed roof without falling, I'd need a running start.

"What's the problem?" Frank shouted. "Need some incentive?"

Frank's face disappeared from the window and a sudden scream rang out in the night air.

"Ashley!" I shouted.

Holding tight to the rifle, I ran across the terrace, jumped and went airborne. My foot caught the edge of the shed roof with less than an inch to spare. Digging my heels in the shingles, I crawled over to the fire escape that led to an entrance on the second floor of the theater. Racing up the steps, I pushed on the door and it creaked open. The place looked darker than a dungeon.

"It's crunch time," the voice in my head reminded. *"You sure you want to go in there? In case you didn't notice, he's crazy. If you don't take him out quick, he's gonna end your breathing habits. You could still turn back. Hightail it back down the fire escape and make a quick getaway."*

I wanted to run, maybe find an easier way to rescue Beth's daughter. We could steal a boat from the harbor in Jersey and float off to some tropical beach and eat fish. Yeah, that sounded just about right.

"Please Eddie, save Ashley," Beth's voice echoed again. *"She doesn't have much time."*

Staring wearily at the door, I stepped inside.

The theater's plush red carpet squished underneath my feet. Switching on my flashlight, I took a look around.

I was in a lobby, the second floor of the building. A concession stand sat in the center of the entranceway that led to a balcony. The theater hadn't been used for weeks but the linoleum around a counter where they served refreshments still felt sticky from soft drinks and alcohol.

Sweat dribbled down my forehead. The air was still. Secretive. Caked with silence. There were no immediate signs of Frank. No worries. The bastard was like a jack in a box; he'd pop up when I least expected it.

"Ashley?" I whispered.

Someone threw a plastic water bottle that landed near my feet. Startled, I whirled around and fired off a round. For an instant I caught a glimpse of Frank's darkened silhouette vanishing around a corner. His footsteps echoed against the empty walls of the theater as he hurried down a staircase.

Moving quickly, I raced after him. At the bottom of the stairs was a reception area and ticket booth. A mass of sunken shadows crouched in every corner of the room.

"Hey cowboy, over here!" Frank's voice boomed near the entrance hall of the theater.

I pulled the trigger again. The bullet hit empty air. Just up ahead, heavy footsteps ran down a corridor.

"Keep it moving," the little voice in my head prodded. *"Don't give him time to breathe."*

Turning down a hall, I walked in the theater, towards the stage. Outside of a few props, the room looked empty.

"Frank?" I cocked the gun's hammer. "Come on out. I got something for you."

Long satin curtains were arranged on either side of the stage. I cautiously stepped behind one of the drapes. I saw a room, probably used for wardrobe changes by actors.

"Ashley?" I jiggled the handle but the door was locked.

I heard someone moan.

"Ashley, is that you?"

"In here!" she shouted.

"Stand clear," I yelled.

Aiming the gun, I shot the lock. The door creaked open. Poised to do damage, I stormed in.

Ashley stood in the corner of the room. Tears spilled down her cheeks. Directly behind her, Frank held her by a clump of straggly hair. Smiling grimly, he dangled a knife at the young girl's throat.

"Leave her go Frank." The gun tightened in my hands.

"You first," he countered. "Hand over the weapon."

"Leave her go now!" I shouted angrily and took aim.

"Maybe you should shoot me," Frank dared. "It's like the old west, Billy the Kid and all that crap. You think you're a quicker than my knife?" He prodded Ashley's neck with the blade. "Draw partner."

"I'll do it."

"Will you? Then show some balls. Pull the trigger."

"I'm telling you I'll shoot."

"Pull it!" Frank demanded. "Pull it or I'll slice the kid open."

I glared and smirked. Ashley was low to the ground. Frank stood up straight. I had a clear headshot. The enemy was scoped. "Say goodbye."

Grinning, I squeezed the trigger but my smile quickly wilted.

The gun made a hollow click.

"Maybe you should have counted your bullets." Frank stared at me with contempt. "I did," he said. "You're empty."

Tossing the rifle, I picked up a metal chair in the corner of the room and barreled forward. Taken off guard, Frank covered up but not before I smashed it against his shoulder. He fell down and dropped the knife. I kicked it across the floor. Ashley slipped from his grasp and crawled to a neutral corner.

Recovering quickly, Frank sprung to his feet. He hit me with a kidney punch followed by a knee to the ribs. I buckled over and gasped.

Limping and bleeding, Frank grabbed Ashley and picked her up, the young girl's limbs flailing as he hurried out the door. Haunting echoes of her cries reverberated off the darkened walls of the theater.

"*Don't stop,*" Beth's haunting voice called. "*Save her Eddie. Save Ashley.*"

Grabbing Frank's knife off the floor, I struggled to my feet and headed for the door.

Out in the corridor, footsteps ran back up a flight of steps that led to the second floor. Hobbling on bruised knees, I trudged back up the steps. Nobody was in the foyer, but a loud scream turned my head towards the balcony entrance. When I ran inside, I nearly banged into Frank, headfirst.

"That's far enough!" he shouted in a commanding tone.

Freezing solid, my eyes widened.

Frank stood by the railing of the balcony. His outstretched arms dangled Ashley over the edge. Streaks of terror dashed down the young girl's face. Her feet thrashed at empty air.

"Don't move or the kid better grow wings fast," he said.

"Stop Frank," I pleaded, holding my hands out. "Let her go. I'm the one you want."

"Here's the problem Eddie." Frank looked tired, crazy. "You didn't adhere to the rules of the game. There are consequences in life, right? People pay when they don't follow protocol."

Ashley twisted in horror. Her breath sounded out in raspy pangs of fright as she looked down at the missing floor beneath her.

"What good would it do to kill the girl?" I tried reasoning. "You got me. Leave her go."

Frank paused and sucked at his lips. "I'll tell you what cowboy. Drop the knife. Get on your knees, hands behind your head."

"Frank, please..."

"I said lose the knife and get down!"

I tossed the knife on the rug and dropped to the floor. "I don't have any other weapons. Satisfied?" I raised my hands. "Now leave her go Frank. Leave her go and I'll do whatever you ask."

"That's always a thought," he considered. "I might need a good dog. Tell me something Eddie. What if I agree to your terms? You gonna do whatever I want?"

"You got it."

"If I say jump, you ask how high, right?"

"You're the boss Frank. Just leave the kid go."

Frank paused and weighed the proposal. Finally his stony face cracked a grin. "I don't think so cowboy. That's not the immediate plan."

Staring coldly, he loosened his grip and dropped Ashley.

38

Falling Down

When I was a kid one of the neighbors, Cooper Sampson, cruised up the alley in a new Corvette that his parents bought him for graduation. A smart grin danced on his lips as he gunned the gas pedal to the floor. He drove full tilt towards a coal bank when the brakes failed. The car flew over the overhang of the embankment, went airborne, rolled down a hill and then landed on its roof, bursting into flames. Sometimes at night when I wake up I can still hear the screams of Cooper as he plunged to his death. It was the same shriek of terror echoing in my ears that I heard from Ashley as she slipped from Frank's grasp.

Frank!"

I lunged forward. Frank balled up his fist and hit me with an uppercut. Staggering backwards, I fell to the floor.

"Get up," he demanded. "I got more for you."

My defenses were worn thin. Still I refused to stay down. If I died, it wouldn't be without a fight.

Getting back on my feet, Frank whirled around and swung. I bent backwards and felt his knuckles swish passed my nose. For a moment he was an open target. Winding up, I slammed my fist into his jaw and followed up with a punch to abdomen. Stumbling, he tripped over a balcony seat and tumbled to the floor but instantly stood back up. Anger cratered his face as he lurched towards me.

"He's on shaky legs," the little guy in my head screamed. *"Take him down now!"*

Rushing forward, I delivered a solid right hook to the jaw and hard punches to the ribs, as if chopping down a big oak. Finally I heard a loud scream and Frank fell to the floor.

"Yes!" I raised my hands.

No.

Frank didn't scream. It was someone else.

I looked around in confusion. The noise came from the edge of the balcony.

Hanging on a wooden baluster, her fingers slipping fast, Ashley cried for help.

Racing over, I reached out my hand. "Grab hold."

Too frightened to move, the young girl's eyes, ghosted with terror, stared at me. After a minute she risked reaching out and grabbed my hand.

"Hang on tight," I told her. "You're gonna be okay."

I started pulling her up but fast moving footsteps approached from behind me. Frank wasn't finished.

Plowing ahead like a wild bull, he struck quick and hard, toppling me over the banister. I grabbed the railing with one hand and held on to Ashley with the other.

Hanging in mid air, I looked up to see Frank's grim face at the edge of the balcony.

"I'll give you this cowboy." He spit blood. "You put up a hell of a fight."

Struggling to hang on, I searched Frank's face for some buried light, a flicker of compassion, but found only holes of blackness overshadowing his soul.

Ashley clung tight around me in a spider-like shape. Her frightened eyes pleaded for deliverance all the while Beth's haunting words whispered in my ear.

"Save her Eddie. Please, save my baby."

Maybe it was true. People see their lives pass before them at the end. For an instant something flashed inside me, as if a warm wind of memories took on a life of their own and blew across the open fields of my mind. For a minute I saw my mother, now gone, smiling down on me from a distant corner of the universe. I could hear the waves and feel my toes scrunch the sand on a summer afternoon on the Jersey shore. I could also sense the heartbreak of losing love and the magic of rekindling it. Life laughs, life cries, life lives and then dies. I could feel all those things as the world, a fleeting cloud underneath my feet, was about to be swept away.

"Don't stop now Eddie." Beth's voice again, loud and determined. *"Save her!"*

I looked down at Ashley. Stark terror circled her face like a raven.

"Let go of the railing," Frank ordered from above.

Peering down, I looked at the floor, two stories below. The fall would kill us. If it didn't, we'd at least break bones and die a slow death in the cold of the darkened theater.

"You listening to me cowboy? I said let go," Frank repeated.

My fingers slipped a little but managed to keep hold of the railing.

"You just got to make things difficult, don't you?" Frank complained. Stooping down, he picked the knife up off the floor that I dropped and positioned it over my wrist. "I'd hate to get medieval here," he said. "Let go of the railing or I'll cut it off."

Despite the threat, instinct outweighed the measure of Frank's terrorism. Decidedly I wanted to stay alive, if for no other reason, Ashley couldn't survive alone. Maybe the day would arrive when the world recovered from the oil disaster. I wanted the kid to be able to put on a prom dress and dance, her face aglow with the promise of dreams. I wanted her to fall in love, you know, get that feeling that makes the whole world right. I wanted her to have a chance.

"You asked for this," said Frank.

Lowering the knife, Frank readied himself for the gruesome particulars but suddenly halted. Winds of confidence shifted direction. He turned around and peered into the darkness with uncertainty.

Near the entrance of the balcony, something moved. A crouching dark figure left out menacing growl.

Shadow had returned, poised to do battle.

Shadow leaned forward. Wrinkles of tension creased the dog's forehead. The corners of his mouth, pulled back tight, exposed a full set of teeth and gums. Judging by the dog's rigid stance, the self-determined mission was clear: take no prisoners.

"You again," said Frank, his voice hesitant.

Shadow growled, eyes cemented on the immediate threat.

"I figured you'd turn up." Frank turned and raised the knife. "I've been waiting for the chance to..."

Frank never finished the sentence.

Shadow leapt in the air. The dog's teeth sunk into his neck. Something underneath Frank's skin cracked as if the animal bit into hard candy.

Groaning, Frank staggered backwards. He jabbed the knife at the animal but the dog was too swift. Shadow rushed forward, bullet fast, and knocked the weapon from his hands. Snapping at Frank's throat, Shadow momentarily backed up, made a throaty growl, and then charged ahead again, ramming into Frank.

Frank's eyes grew threefold. He flapped his arms and tried to keep his balance. Finally he toppled over the railing, his limbs thrashing in mid air as he spiraled down and crashed against the floor with a dull thud.

39

Dark Places

"Hang on!" I shouted to Ashley. Gripping the broken banister, I pulled myself up to solid ground. Ashley clung tight around my waist. Her eyes, measured in waves of terror, were pasted shut and too afraid to look down.

Finally I mustered enough strength to throw both arms over the top of the railing. It creaked as if weakening but held together long enough for me to drag both myself and the girl back to stable ground. Shadow trotted over and wagged a long tail. Rolling over on my back, I gasped for air but still smiled. We were cut and bleeding but still alive.

After a minute, I leaned up on bruised elbows and looked at Ashley. Shivering, the young girl folded her hands at her sides and turned her sneakers inward, almost as if closing herself up in a protective shell where the world couldn't reach her. A smudge of dirt on her cheek, she pinched her eyes shut, almost as if too frightened to open them. Her face ghosted with fear, she breathed in quick sharp gasps.

"You're safe now," I said softly.

Her bottom lip trembled. She wiped at her nose and said, "I'm scared mister. Can you help me find my mom?" She fidgeted from foot to foot.

How do you answer a question like that? How do you explain to an eight year old kid that everything she had ever known, that innocent place where mothers read bedtime stories and little girls played with dolls, was gone.

"Ashley." I paused. "There was an accident."

"An accident?"

"Something happened."

"I don't understand."

Getting to my feet, I trudged over to the girl and squatted down. "I tried to help her. There was nothing I could do."

"Don't say that mister." Misty tears spilled down Ashley's cheeks. "Please don't say that."

My heart broke for the kid. I reached out to hold her but she pulled back. Any crumbs of trust that she once had for people had now grown stale and were swept away in the wind.

"I'm afraid she's gone," I said quietly.

"That's not true!" she shouted.

"I'm sorry Ashley. There was an explosion and then..." I couldn't finish the words.

The kid stared with pouty lips. "Please mister." She stepped forward and tugged at my shirt. "She's alive."

"I know this hurts," I told her. "I tried to change things. I swear I tried."

"Please mister. You've got to listen. She's in the dark place!" Ashley blurted out.

I stopped cold. "What?"

"The bad man." Glancing down at Frank she shuddered. "He locked me in the basement of the hotel. Then after awhile he came back with my mom."

"What are you saying Ashley?"

"He took her out of the room before it exploded."

My heart jumped.

"Afterwards he took us here, to the theater, and put my mom in the dark place. My mom said to tell you that. Please mister." She tugged at my shirt. "She said to tell you. She said you'd know where the dark place is."

My mind reeled in all directions. There were dark places in the world. Beth sometimes talked about them. Standing there in the theater, the haunting presence of Frank creeping over the walls, I thought back in time and the memories washed over me.

Nearing graduation, I bought tickets to *A Streetcar Named Desire*, a drama written by Tennessee Williams and his vivid portrayal of desperate and forsaken characters. The show was at the Opera House, a vaudeville-era playhouse in the center of town. Wind chimes hung in the windows and sang in the warm summer breeze.

Beth looked beautiful that night. She wore a floral print top, pleated black skirt and white sandals. It took some nerve, but finally I put my arm around her. She smiled and cuddled into my shoulder.

"Stay close," she whispered in my ear when the house lights fell. "I get frightened in dark places. Remember when I told you I got lost in the theater?"

I stared at her.

"When I was a young girl, my parents brought me here," she said, a distant look on her face. "It was October. A local theater group decorated the place like a haunted house. Ghosts, goblins, you name it. I accidentally wandered off and got lost." She touched my hand and I melted. "Eddie, there are rooms underneath the building. A trap door on the stage leads to them. They look like catacombs."

I heard stories about the rooms underneath the theater but assumed they were hearsay. A man named Addison Hutton designed and built the place nearly 150 years ago. Hutton claimed it was his crowning achievement in life. Rumor had it that he was buried in a crypt beneath the structure.

"You really think there's a morgue?" I asked.

"It sounds crazy, right? I'm not really sure what all was down there. It was dark," she said. "Really dark. I couldn't have been there more than a few minutes until security found me, still it felt like hours. At times I still have nightmares about it." She paused and stared. "It's almost as if it was a forewarning of something to come."

Reaching up, I gently ran my fingers through her hair. "You don't need to worry about dark places."

"Promise?" Her half lidded eyes rolled up to look at me.

I slipped my arm tight around her waist. Her small frame melted warmly against my chest. Whispering in her ear I said, "I'll keep you safe, no matter what."

40

Shattered Pieces

Sometimes I wonder about life's grand design. We meet people. Go places. Do things. Most of those things seem irrelevant. Often it isn't until weeks, months, or maybe years later that we comprehend the significance of our circumstances. A seed planted in our past grows until one day, when everything is ready, it blooms. That's how I viewed Beth. The story she told me about getting trapped in a room underneath the theater, the *dark place* as she referred to it, wasn't so much a happenstance as a foreshadowing of the future.

"Are you listening mister?" Ashley tugged frantically at arm. "We need to hurry."

Shining the flashlight over the side of the balcony, the muddy light came to rest on Frank's twisted body. His legs appeared broken. Still he offered a slight groan, alerting me to the idea that he wasn't quite dead.

"Wait here. Keep the dog with you," I whispered and patted Shadow on the head. "I'll be right back."

Racing down the stairs, I turned left and walked into the audience hall. Frank lay collapsed on the floor. Despite his injuries, his shallow breath rose and fell in the stillness of the theater. Sidestepping him, I flinched when his hand moved ever so slightly.

If Beth's story was accurate, I'd find a trap door on the stage that led to a number of passages beneath the building. Climbing up on stage, sure enough, I found what I was looking for over by the orchestra pit. A door that lifted up was built into the stage floor. No doubt it served as an entry for scenic changes or access for actors to the performance area. Pulling the trap door up, I bent down and peered inside.

Underneath the stage, a corridor extended nearly the entire length of the building. Old lighting and sound equipment was stacked up in the hall along with some mannequins, a skeleton, and other props.

"Beth, are you in there?" I called but nobody answered.

With a last glance at Frank's unmoving body, I stepped inside.

The place smelled musty, and the dark, impenetrable. Cobwebs raked the air; twice I flinched and batted them away from my eyes. On the back wall of the room, someone took a can of red spray paint and scribbled the words, *BROADWAY or BUST*, across the plasterboard.

Glancing around, the flashlight beam settled on an open door at the end of the hall. I walked slowly towards it, expecting to find another dressing room and stage props. Inside the small room, walls with cracked plaster revealed exposed boards and rafters. Dried mortar fell from the ceiling and littered the floor.

There was also a wretched stench, a mixture of rotted wood and mildewed air. The smell probably came from dampness trapped in close quarters. Still given Beth's account of the dark place, I couldn't shake the feeling that the rancid odor emanated from a long dead corpse in a constant state of decomposition.

"Beth?" I whispered, almost fearing I'd wake the dead.

There was still no answer. It occurred to me that Frank might have moved Beth, or in a grimmer scenario, killed her and left the remains behind, a permanent resident of the theater's subterranean world.

Walking further, there were more rooms. Some of them were empty, and others, filled with tarps and trinkets, undoubtedly used for theatrical settings.

Turning around, a coffin constructed of cardboard with a plastic mannequin in it made me gasp and drop the flashlight. When it hit the ground, the light went out.

"Damn-it!" I scoured the floor, found it, and picked it back up. Tapping the light against my leg, it still wouldn't turn on.

Near the trap door, a noise caught my attention. At first I thought it might be a trickle of water dripping from the ceiling. However, this sounded different. Someone shuffled around in the darkness.

"Beth, is that you?" I called softly.

All corners of the room remained voiceless. For an instant the sadistic face of Frank emerged in the shadowy recesses of my mind. His injuries from the fall off the balcony should have been fatal, or at the very least, rendered him a permanent cripple. I wasn't sure about that though. Crazy people sometimes had unlimited strength. I once read where some idiot on PCP took several bullets to the chest but still beat the hell out of a couple of police officers on the Santa Monica freeway.

I remained quiet. That proved difficult. Even the slightest move made noise in the tightly packed silence. The darkness ran deep but still I felt someone's eyes watching me.

Bending down and feeling around, I picked a chunk of mortar up off the floor.

"Who's there?" I asked. "Show yourself."

A dark figure brushed against a wall, not more than a few feet ahead of me. I could hear them breathing.

"Answer or I'll..."

"You'll do what?" the voice in my head returned for some last minute counseling. *"Hello? Are you listening close? Let me spell it out. You got no gun."*

Turning around, I swung my fist and tried hitting an invisible target but struck empty air. Jiggling the flashlight again, this time it lit. Clutching the mortar tight, I charged ahead to finish the score.

41

Coming Out of the Dark

I abruptly stopped and stared in confusion.

"Beth?"

Huddled in a corner near the back of a room and rocking in place, Beth peered into nothingness. Wringing her hands together, she slapped at her arms as if warding off a nest of spiders feeding on damp skin. If it wasn't for her blue eyes, distant and fearful, I might not have recognized her at all.

"It's me, Eddie." I took a slow step.

"Don't come any closer!" She flinched and jerked backwards.

Looking down at her hand, my eyes widened. Possibly from a storage shed and careless gardener, she gripped an axe, only instead of a cardboard prop, this one was real. Although rusted, the blade still appeared edgy and sharp.

Dropping the chunk of mortar, I raised my hands. "Take it easy. I'm here to help."

Uncertainty muddied her expression. The weapon trembled in her fingers.

"Put it down Beth," I told her. "I won't hurt you."

"Yes you will!" she shouted, her skin tense, clammy. "You want to kill me." Refusing to disarm, fear twitched in her fingertips.

"Don't do this Beth. I'm not the enemy," I told her. "I'm not Frank."

The mere mention of Frank drew a veil of terror over Beth's eyes. I had no idea what cruelties she endured at his hands. Still before the world tipped over like a huge plastic ball, Beth had a normal life. But those special moments in the sun, like raising a daughter, had fallen off a mantel and shattered to pieces. Forget reasoning. I'd be lucky to escape alive.

"Please put it down." I stared at the axe.

I could see it in her eyes. She didn't hear a word. Maybe it was a lack of food and water or perhaps Frank's beastly presence, but rational thoughts in Beth's mind turned alien and befuddled. I was no longer the man who rescued her from the hands of a killer; I was a threat bent on terminating her life.

"Drop the axe," I repeated, this time more loudly.

She stared at me. Her face was painted with dread. Curling her fingers tightly around the axe, she suddenly swung fiercely. I ducked and the blade cut into empty air. Fast and furious, she moved in wielding the weapon. Backing up, I tripped and fell to the floor.

"Beth!" I shouted.

Rather than recollection, fear and defense shielded her mind and body. She stood over me, the axe's handle crunched in her fist. Any semblance of rational thought hadn't just been compromised; it was nonexistent. Raising the weapon for a fatal blow, she stopped at the sound of approaching footsteps.

———

"Mommy?"

Beth whirled around. The axe trembled in her hand.

"Mommy, don't!" Alarm rang in Ashley's voice. "It's me." Tears flooded her eyes. "It's Ashley."

Beth paused. Confusion shadowed her face. She glanced at the axe, almost as if surprised to find it there. A second later she let it slide from her fingers and fall to the ground. Crumbling to her knees, Beth put her head in her hands and began to cry.

"I'm so sorry baby," she glanced at Ashley through trembling fingers.

Stepping forward, the young girl fell into the arms of her mother.

Breathing heavy, I crawled over to Beth. Madness, a fog lifting after a long hard rain, cleared from her face. Instead of a restless sea, the calmness of her blue eyes, the ones I fell in love with a long time ago, returned. Reaching out, she put her arms around me and pulled me close.

"Thank you Eddie," she mouthed the words. "You saved her. You saved Ashley."

I thought about. I thought about it hard as we sat there in a room underneath the theater and held each other in the dark. I thought about the many things we'd been through, all the things the world had become, and all the terrible walls of injustice that fell around us. Looking at Beth and Ashley, after the nightmares we endured, the crosses we bore, I couldn't help but to wonder how I might keep these people, this new family of mine, safe in a world gone mad.

Beth touched my hand. "Please tell me Frank is gone," she said softly. "Please tell me it's over now."

Stroking her hair and staring into the darkness, finally I answered, "Almost."

42

A Night at the Opera

Frank's eyes blinked open. Blood and grime stained his shirt. Looking down, he stared at his shattered leg and groaned. Leaning against the back wall of the theater, he tried to stand, grunted, and then slumped back down in a sitting position.

"It's no use Frank." I stood there and pointed the Remington. "You're busted up."

Looking from side to side, he said, "Where am I?"

"It's not the Waldorf in New York."

"So now you're a comedian." Frank glared and glanced at the rifle. "Still packing an empty gun?"

I remained stock still. "I found bullets. You had them hid with the rest of your stash in the theater's supply room."

Outside, the whoosh of a helicopter flew overtop the theater.

"Listen to that, sweet Jesus." Frank grimaced as he tilted his head in the air. "It sounds like the cavalry."

I took a step closer and leaned down. "Not for you Frank."

Pausing uncertainly, he stared at me. "So what now cowboy, you gonna kill me?"

Frank's legs were twisted and useless, still he frightened me. Maybe I watched too many horror movies as a kid. After all, evil always finds a way to come back.

"We all got to adhere to the laws of the jungle, right Frank?" I told him.

"Jungles are for lions." Frank clenched his teeth and fingered the wound on his shoulder. Sweat, mixed with dirt and blood, rolled down his cheek. "You're no killer Eddie," he said. "You're a starved sparrow, too afraid to fly south for the winter. If you were planning a murder, you would have done it already."

Thinking about it, I didn't know if I could kill someone in cold blood, even a man like Frank. That surprised me. Put a person in a hostile environment and either he'll die or learn how to kill quickly and without conscience. Ever since the oil disaster began, I lived like an animal. I ate from trashcans and hid behind boarded up windows. The tank on my moral reserve had gone empty weeks ago. Still I wanted to believe that somewhere, anywhere, a glimmer of sunlight shined and that something good remained in the world. I still wanted to have faith in things like falling in love, and that maybe, just maybe, a kid like Ashley would have a chance for a good life instead of a struggle for survival in some dark and hopeless hole.

At the same time a fire burned inside of me. It was as if a well trained surgeon had cut away all traces of empathy, leaving me bankrupt of any sense of moral compassion. I wanted to kill Frank. I wanted it so bad I could taste the blood. Still, standing there with the hammer cocked, I couldn't quite pull the trigger.

"Just as I thought." Frank said. "Murder is an art but you're no Leonardo Da Vinci. Take it from someone who knows cowboy. You can always tell a killer by their eyes. They're hungry. Dry as funeral drums. There's no hate, no compassion, no nothing. He's that guy in the courtyard pulling the switch on an electric chair. The place stinks of death, but does he notice?

He's just living the moment, a drunk on a barstool staring into an empty glass. That's a killer's world, and if something gets in his way? He removes it." He glanced up at the ceiling as another helicopter flew by. "If you think you got that inside of you, then go ahead," he taunted. "Shoot me."

Staring at him I finally said, "You don't understand Frank."

"I don't understand what?" He snapped back.

Pausing, I answered, "I never said that I was the one who was going to kill you."

Turning my head, Beth walked through the door.

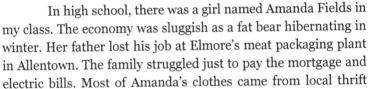

In high school, there was a girl named Amanda Fields in my class. The economy was sluggish as a fat bear hibernating in winter. Her father lost his job at Elmore's meat packaging plant in Allentown. The family struggled just to pay the mortgage and electric bills. Most of Amanda's clothes came from local thrift shops. She didn't enjoy the chic luxuries of some of her peers, nor did she get asked to high school dances or the senior prom.

Even back then I realized that kids often thrived on that kind of adversity. Mostly there were two forms of life that roamed school halls; the one was the hopeless loser who ate all alone in the cafeteria and never got called when choosing sides for basketball.

The other form of life, primal as wolves, traveled in packs and fought for positions of superiority. They were determined to keep the Amanda Fields of the world submersed under water, never giving them a chance to breathe. If someone like Amanda put on perfume, pinned her hair up and went to a dance, her adversaries would become furious, even hateful, at the thought of someone trying to escape the trenches of life.

Linda Beers, captain of the cheerleading squad, spent much of her days taunting people of a lesser god. She thrived on dominance and hair spray, taunting the less fortunate and using them as a stepping stone to climb the ladder of social success.

"Hey hillbilly." Linda glanced up and down Amanda's shabby jeans and second hand blouse. "You're in my seat." Linda looked around, searching for an audience, including Dale Price, the cute guy from Mathematics 101.

Wanting to avoid an argument, Amanda picked up her lunch tray and started walking away.

"Not so fast," said Linda. "You broke my rules." Grabbing a milk carton, she threw it in Amanda's face.

Startled, Amanda dropped her lunch tray. Jeers and laughter erupted in the cafeteria.

Amanda's cheeks turned beet red. Anger fused with fear saturated her every emotion. She shot Linda Beers a hateful glare.

Linda laughed. "Look who has a chip on her shoulder." She glanced at Amanda's shoes. "Try a new image. You know, lose the clodhoppers and wear some decent clothes?" She stepped back. "Oh, I forgot. You're father doesn't work. A welfare recipient, right?"

The problem was this; some lines you don't cross. Families are one of them. When you do, the glass fills up. It overflows. That's how I saw Amanda that day, filled up and overflowing. She had been belittled and preyed upon. Now that person was coming after her father, someone she respected, someone she loved and someone who loved her. Suddenly the glass tipped over and shattered on the floor.

Amanda rushed forward. She tackled Linda Beers to the ground. Balling up a petite but sturdy fist, she crunched the girl's nose, again and again. The beating might have gone on forever if Mr. Perry, the school's music teacher, didn't drag the girl's apart.

There is a place where basic principles and fear of predators disintegrate. Something snaps. People like Amanda Fields, whatever the consequence, stand up to be heard.

In that dark theater, in a world gone crazy, that's what I saw in Beth as she stepped through the door. Her eyes were targeted, uncompromising, and deadly. As Frank watched her slow approach, for the first time in a long time, a shadow of fear crossed his face.

Beth's cold stare could have stopped a bullet. She walked straight towards Frank. Crunching down on her knees, she stared directly in his eyes.

Frank stiffened. Reservation scribbled his face. "I see you survived the catacombs." Regardless of his compromised position, he remained cool and in control.

"You hurt me." She glared. A vine of hate grew in her voice, not from fear but rage. "Even worse, you hurt my daughter and killed innocent people."

Frank lowered his eyes and then raised them again. "It's a crazy world," he said. "Let me ask you, do you think you're the only person to get hurt? Take a look at me." He glanced at his shattered legs. "You think I deserve this? So I made a few mistakes. I'll bet you didn't have a father that beat you bloody with a steel buckle."

Beth halted Frank with an angry slap. "I don't care Frank," she assured him in a low threatening tone. "Excuses won't save you."

Forcing a grin, Frank met her unsuppressed stare. "Think you're scaring me? You'll have to do better than that."

Crunching up her fist, knuckle tight, Beth struck again. The force of the blow whipped Frank's head around.

"I don't remember asking you to talk," she said. Turning around, Beth picked up a wooden club that was on the floor, perhaps used as a prop in one of the theater productions. She stared coldly at him. "Do we have an understanding?"

Hatred overshadowed Frank's face.

"Tell me something Frank," she asked, slowly turning the club in her hand. "Do you believe in God?" she said. "I'd suggest that you do. I'd suggest that you start talking to him real hard."

Frank's raspy breath grew short. He turned towards me. Urgency shadowed his eyes. "Hey cowboy," he said. "You gonna stand there and let her commit murder? You're big on American justice. If you let her do this, hell, you're as bad as she is; an accessory to a crime."

I stood there quiet and thoughtful, a witness to an execution waiting for the final switch to be pulled.

Beth suddenly dropped the club. Walking over, she grabbed the rifle from my hands, cocked the hammer and shoved it against Frank's throat.

"How does it feel Frank? How does it feel to know your fate is in someone else's hands," she paused, "someone like me?" "Bang bang." She squeezed the trigger.

Frank recoiled. The gun made an empty click rather than a sharp bang.

Beth leaned over him. "I just wanted you to know how it is to be on the receiving end of a bullet," she said in a quiet voice. "But there's worse things in the world than being shot, isn't there?"

Frank's fear was only superseded by his measure of hate. He didn't like being pushed, especially by a woman, even if it meant dying. "You can rot in hell," he shouted at Beth, the cords of his neck standing straight out.

"I know," she said. "You'd love to kill me right now, wouldn't you? I can see it in your eyes. You'd strangle me. In fact, you'd continue tightening the rope even after I took my last breath."

"You think you're intimidating me?" Frank forced a grin. "You're the one that should be worried. Sooner or later I'll get out of here. When I do? I'll kill you and your daughter, and as for you cowboy?" He turned to me. "You'll have the pleasure of watching me take them apart."

Beth looked over at me and then down at Frank. "I'm not going to have my daughter, or me, or anyone else, looking over our shoulders for the rest of our lives. Do you understand Frank?"

Frank's face, sneering and malicious, glared hatefully. "I guess some things in life you just have to live with, right sweetheart?"

Beth paused. "No Frank, not anymore." Raising the rifle, she brought it down hard on his head.

43

A Cowboys Last Stand

Accompanied by Beth and her daughter, I left Frank unconscious on the floor. I could only imagine what might have happened next inside his twisted mind and darkened chambers of the theater. The only thing certain was that terror had been stacked on our shoulders and the final stand had arrived. So if I had to guess Frank's thoughts, I suppose it would go this way.

Frank woke up in the cold confines of the theater, isolated and alone. A flashlight sat on his grungy trousers, just above a badly fractured leg. Breathing at a rapid pace, a mood of dread crawled over his clammy skin.

"You out there cowboy?" he shouted, his voice echoing in the darkness. Picking up the flashlight, he shined it against empty walls. The theater appeared vacant.

Biting back the pain from his wounds, his mind couldn't help but to trail off in disbelief. Eddie Slate, a goddamn car salesman who wouldn't last an hour in the state pen without getting a shank stuck in his throat, had beaten him at his own game.

Frank glanced at his shoulder. A bloodstain, bursting like a flower, sopped his shirt. Among other things, the dog had bitten him, bone deep. He'd need antibiotics, not to mention a good surgeon with a needle and thread.

Still bleeding from the shoulder wasn't the major concern. Falling off the balcony did far more damage. His left leg, numb and lacerated, was bent crooked. The right one, judging by the pain, was severely fractured. Without help, he wasn't going anywhere soon.

Another helicopter flew over top of the building. The boys in uniform must have been making a sweep and checking out the perimeter. If he got lucky, they'd do a house to house search and look for survivors. He'd get rescued. Once they ran his I.D. he'd probably end up in some backwoods detainment center ringed with barbed wire. But after his wounds healed, he'd get out. He'd get out and find that sorry son of a bitch, Eddie Slate, not to mention Beth and her brat daughter. Payback would be expensive. In fact, it would be deadly.

"You hear me?" His voice echoed in the empty theater. "This isn't over!"

Frank froze when he heard a noise coming from beside him on the floor. Turning his head, he saw a radio.

"Hey Frank," a familiar voice sounded out. "Pickup if you're there."

Gritting his teeth, Frank grabbed the radio and held it to his lips. "If it isn't the cowboy," he said, defiant as ever. "I suppose you think you've won. I heard helicopters. You gonna get the military police to haul my ass away and then everyone lives happily ever after?"

"No Frank. There'll be no cops or witnesses."

"You better listen, and listen close." Anger flared in Frank's voice. "I'm gonna get out of this, and when I do, I'll..."

"You'll do what Frank? You gonna come after me? You gonna put a bullet in my head like you did that kid in front of the American Hotel? In case you didn't notice, your legs are broke. You're not going anywhere."

Frank shifted his weight, but any movement, even an inch, brought hot cauldrons of pain. If he could manage to get to his feet, even if he could limp a little, he'd go after Slate and kill him. He'd kill all of them. Still any attempt to reposition his limbs delivered a lesson in agony. He was trapped.

"So what now?" he asked. "You gonna come back, guns blazing, or just leave me rot until the authorities turn up."

"Neither Frank. I got to tell you. You're resourceful as a cat."

Frank stared at the radio.

"While you were knocked out on the carpet, I took a look around. I found your supplies in the theater's upstairs storage closet. That terrorist you met in jail must have really had the black market cornered on weapons. Dynamite. Guns. You got enough explosives stockpiled to blowup Central Park. I even found a timer hooked to a block of C4. I'm just a lousy car salesman, but my guess is that you were gonna use that one on me."

"What's your point cowboy?" Frank stared brutally.

Another pause on the radio. "Take a look above you."

Frank's eyes rolled up and widened. Wired to a rafter, a timer that counted down from seven minutes had been connected to a detonator and a block of C4. All remnants of self-satisfaction that lingered on Frank's face suddenly melted away. Desperation swam in his expression. He tried to move his legs. Using his arms for leverage, for a minute he pulled himself up to a near standing position. But his legs, broken stilts, hampered any hope of escape. He slid back down to the floor.

"Let me out of here!" he demanded, pounding his fist against a wall.

"Is something wrong Frank?"

"I said let me out!"

"I know. You're frightened. I don't blame you. Dying isn't easy. Just ask the people you killed. You might take Beth's advice. Start praying."

"I don't believe in God," Frank shot back boldly.

"Trust me. Tie an atheist to a railroad track with a train coming? He'll pray."

"This is murder," Frank charged. "You really want to be labeled a killer? What, you want me to beg? You win cowboy. Get me out of here. I'll give you all your supplies back and more. We can make a deal."

"All deals are done Frank. Now you should take some time alone, maybe think about all the things that happened, all the things you've done. There's still time to do that." A pause on the radio. "About seven minutes of it."

And the radio clicked off.

44

Boom

"What the hell?" Corporal Neal craned his neck out the window of the chopper. "Did you see that?" He pointed and turned to Sergeant Mills. "You'd swear the San Andres fault just cracked."

The helicopter shimmied as the force of the explosion blew out windows in surrounding houses.

"Over there." Sergeant Mills peered through his binoculars. The blast came from a building down in the historic district. "Whatever it was turned the whole damn building into rubble."

"Man." Corporal Neal whistled. "I haven't seen a discharge like that since my stint in the Gulf."

A sound on the radio diverted Mills' attention.

"Hello?" Tangled in static, a desperate voice called. "Can anyone hear me?"

Sergeant Mills picked up the receiver. "Mills speaking. Who is this?"

"Eddie," someone answered. "Eddie Slate."

Mills tilted his head and scratched his chin. He vaguely recognized the name. Slate had been broadcasting earlier on the radio. Shifting his binoculars, he again looked at a plume of smoke billowing up from the demolished building. "Something just detonated," he said. "It must have taken out half the block."

A pause on the radio. "Can you see that from your position?" asked Eddie.

"Sure can," said Mills. "We're in a chopper, not more than a click or two away."

"We're not far from you. Can you help us?"

"Afraid not Slate," Mills answered. "Most of our troops are locked down in the metropolitan areas." Mills shoved a wad of Redman chew tobacco in his mouth. "We're living in desperate times. Buckle down and hang tight comrade. We're gonna..."

"Wait!" Eddie shouted over the radio. "Please, we have no food, no water. We've got a little girl with us. You can't be far off. I can hear the helicopter."

Sergeant Mills scanned the parameter with his binoculars. Just ahead, near some railroad tracks, he saw movement. There was a man with a woman and a young girl, not to mention a dog. Man, he hadn't seen a dog around in weeks. The guy carried the little girl in one arm and hung tight to the woman's waist with the other. They appeared to be headed towards the bridge that led to the east end of town.

"That you down there on the railroad tracks?" asked Mills.

"That's us." Eddie stopped and waved his arms.

Staring intently, Mills finally tapped the pilot on the shoulder. "See that clearing over by those trees?" He pointed at a vacant parking lot. "Put her down for a minute."

Corporeal Neal blinked uncertainly. "Headquarters gave strict orders, observation only."

Mills looked in his binoculars again. Exhausted, Eddie Slate dropped to his knees, never letting go of the little girl cradled in his arms.

Sucking at his lips thoughtfully he finally said, "Forget headquarters. You know what they say. What happens in Vegas."

The pilot made a slow descent. The helicopter touched down in the middle of the parking lot, the whirling blades beating the night air into submission. Mills jumped out, spit a wad of chew tobacco on the ground and trudged over to where Eddie stood.

"Eddie Slate?"

Eddie nodded. "Thank God you guys made it."

"Don't thank him too much." Sergeant Mills pulled a water bottle off his belt and passed it to him. "We're only here on a surveillance mission. Our orders say to check the parameter and then head for home." Mills bent down at patted the dog on the head.

Leaning over, Eddie set Ashley down and handed the water bottle to Beth. "We haven't had any news in weeks," he said. "What's going on out there?"

"What isn't?" Mills answered. "The economy is gone, warships have refineries surrounded in the Gulf, the cities are rioting and 250 million pissed off Americans turned vigilante are ready to kill for a loaf of bread. Read the Revelations. You'll get the picture."

"Please," said Eddie. "You've got to get us out of here."

"Not gonna happen." Sergeant Mills shook his head. "Besides, we got no place to take you. Unless you're an elected official with a ticket to a political fallout shelter, everyone is sailing on the Titanic these days."

Sergeant Mills heard a slight whimper and glanced down at Ashley. Her chin trembled. Tears rimmed her eyes. Pulling her coat tight, she shivered in the frigid temperatures.

"I'm so cold mommy."

"It's okay sweetheart." Beth cuddled her close.

Reaching up, Sergeant Mills touched his shirt pocket. He carried a crinkled photo of his wife and daughter around ever since the oil disaster began. His family lived on a base back in Dover, supposedly secure. But looking over the landscape these last few weeks? Every time he got called out on surveillance, from the cities to the rural areas, he wondered what he'd find when he got back.

Sergeant Mills turned to Eddie. "Listen to me," he said. "I had an army buddy named Ivan Dunham. Just after everything went to hell, he got shot in a firefight during an insurgence down around Charleston. Ivan was a banana when it came to survival. He swore we'd get nuked by some foreign power and built a bomb shelter in his basement. It's filled with food, ammunition, you name it. He could have fought Normandy from his cellar." Mills paused and looked at Ashley. Pulling out a scrap of paper, he jotted something down and handed it to Eddie. "This is what you're gonna do Slate. Go to this address. It won't be visible, but there should be an opening in one of the basement walls that leads to an underground shelter."

Eddie stared and blinked at the paper. "Are you sure?"

"Trust me," Sergeant Mills said. "I've been there. If nobody found the place, you should have enough supplies to make it through the winter. With any luck things will have gotten better by then."

Holding Ashley close, Beth looked up at the sergeant. "Thank you." She nodded her head.

"Consider it a holiday gift," Mills said.

"What do you mean?" Eddie tilted his head.

"It's Christmas Eve pal, Santa and all that crap." Sergeant Mills stared into the icy darkness. Again he touched the picture in his shirt pocket. "Remember Christmas, church bells and lighted trees? Sometimes that seems like a lifetime ago." Turning to leave, he started walking but then turned around. "Watch your back. Crazy isn't exactly a contained element these days."

"We've been through a lot," Eddie said over the swooshing sound of helicopters.

"Hey Slate," Mills shouted. "That's almost all behind you now." Reaching down, he ruffled Ashley's hair. Walking across the lot, he hoisted himself back inside the open door of the chopper. "Take your family and get to safety. Stay low on the radar," he shouted as the rotary blade spun faster and the helicopter lifted off, fading into the night sky.

From Eddie Slate's Diary
101 Violins

It's been three months since the world we once knew ended. Looking back, it didn't really matter if it was an oil famine, a nuclear war, an asteroid strike or a solar flare. The results were all the same. Sometimes I think the real enemy has been society's stubborn refusal to look at the obvious. Instead of gassing up the cars we should have been weaning ourselves off a steady diet of CRUDE. We had the technology; we just didn't have the foresight, and the crisis caught us with a good left hook when we didn't expect it.

Most of the information I get these days is from drifters, ghosts who walk the highways from city to city. The other day I met a guy named Melvin who told me he bicycled all the way from Rhode Island.

"Not much changed, especially in places like New York and Baltimore." Melvin scratched at the scruff under his chin. Pulling out a bent cigarette, he lit up. "People got nothing to eat. Peddling up the PA turnpike I found three bodies in front of a food barn at a rest station. With no hospitals or clean water, there's a lot of illness too. The Center for Disease Control can't restrain it. Someone even told me that FEMA is burning bodies at local dumps."

I looked at him quizzically. "You're joking, right?"

"Trust me. All the late night hosts like Craig Ferguson have left the house. There are no comedians left in the world." The wind blew and he pulled a shabby grey coat tight around himself. "You can bet your ass the fighter jets are in the air guarding barrels of Crude and making contingency plans for a hostile incursion to get whatever of the stuff is holed up in the world."

That pretty much punctuated people's attitudes. With communications down, it was impossible to know if and where the bombs dropped.

Sporting crew cuts and stern attitudes, the military eventually showed up in town. Just last week I heard a soldier shot someone who tried to rob a man at knifepoint for food rations. Otherwise, law enforcement is nearly nonexistent. To compensate for the lack of it, some of the locals banded together, the reason being? There's force in numbers. Instead of one nation under God, civilization has been reduced to tribes and vigilantes, traveling in packs like wild dogs, desperate to survive.

On a brighter note, just the other day I saw a small miracle. A young Scottish girl in her twenties and nine months pregnant went into labor right in front of Chelsea's Market. People came out of their houses carrying blankets and pillows to keep her warm. Jeremy Sterner, a pre-med student who worked as a dishwasher at Camille's Café before the crisis hit, kneeled down on the sidewalk in front of her.

"That's it," he told the girl. "Push hard. You can do it."

The girl's face twisted in tears of both pain and joy.

"One more time," Jeremy urged. "I can see the head." A smile the size of Texas spread over his lips. "Push harder."

A baby girl suddenly cried and another life entered the world. You don't know what that sounded like. Maybe you think you do, but in a world where people kill each other for scraps of food, hearing that baby? It was music from heaven with 101 violins playing in the background.

As things turned out, Sergeant Mills was right. Gathering what little supplies we had, Beth, Ashley and myself, not to mention Shadow, trekked to a neighboring town where Ivan Dunham lived. In his basement, I found a concealed entranceway that had been covered over with plywood and led to an underground shelter. We found food, bottled water, guns, and even a vented kerosene heater with plenty of fuel. I'll never see Sergeant Mills again, but I'll also never forget when he landed a helicopter in a parking lot on one Christmassy night, and for all practical purposes, saved all of our lives.

Regardless of the passing weeks, it remains dangerous outside. Ashley spends most of her time playing with Shadow, the dog that rescued us on that bleak night when we faced off against a monster named Frank. Otherwise, we stay in the shelter awaiting the spring thaw which has now begun to arrive.

I talked it over with Beth. We decided that in the coming weeks, we'd take our chances on the road and head south. Who knows? Maybe we'll find a little deserted oceanfront property along the coast in warmer climates. The fishing is good, and besides, I miss the sound of ocean waves.

Sometimes I get a little stir crazy. The other day I hiked up the road and sat by the Mauch Chunk Lake in Thorpe. Now in early April, birds sing and ripples of water shimmer in the morning sun. Sometimes in those quiet moments, I reminisce about the days before the oil disaster invaded all of our lives. I look back like an old man, tired and worn but full of memories.

Other times aren't quite so happy. I have nightmares about Frank and the terrible struggles we endured to survive. Beth gently rubs my head and holds me close during those instances, and suddenly, even in the darkness, I see a ray of sunlight shining through the window of my life.

I see that same ray whenever I look into the innocent blue eyes of a little girl named Ashley or feel the warm touch of Beth's head cuddling against my shoulder, deep in the night. I make both of them feel safe; they make me feel invincible. In those beautiful moments, I'm reminded that even after all the punches thrown by this thing called life, I could still hear the echoes of children's laughter tumbling in green fields. I think most of all, after all the heartache, all the pain, I'm reminded that love still matters. In fact, it matters more than ever.

I have no idea where we'll go from here, although I am certain of one thing; the old saying is true. Life isn't about all the years you live or how many breaths you take. It's about what you do with those breaths along the way, no matter how short or long that time is in the world.

As I sit here, a candle flickering on the table and Beth quietly sleeping on my shoulder with Ashley, I know that somehow we'll go on, just as I know more than ever, life is about fighting for all the things you believe in and a future waiting to be born.

The End

About the Author

J.L. Davis resides in Jim Thorpe Pennsylvania, Gateway to the Poconos. In his early twenties he worked as everything from a bartender to a musician playing drums on the local circuit between hiatuses to the ocean.

Author of such satire novels as *NESTING with the LOONS,* Currently he's working on his next novel.

OTHER BOOKS
by J.L. Davis include:

From the critically acclaimed satire novel,
NESTING with the LOONS
writing as Jeff Davis

"With its acid edge and wicked humor, Jeff Davis's rapid fire depiction of bureaucracy gone wild digs underneath the fingernails of the typical blue collar worker, satirizing both modern-day relationships and business life. Specifically, if we can't stand our jobs and families, live for the day to escape!

Luckless in love and trapped in a dead end job, Jack Snaggler thinks his fortune is about to change when he meets a drop-dead gorgeous brunette named Paradise at a local bar. Think again. When a shady fast food chef goes missing and coworkers start disappearing, Jack finds himself being framed for murder. If he wants to stay alive long enough to ever see Paradise again, he'll first need to escape a conspiracy, that at each turn, involves almost everyone he knows.

"Part dysfunctional love interest, part corporate mindset, and part 60's cool, the road to paradise has never been so tainted or hilarious."

~ Readerman's Bookshelf

From the satire, *NESTING with the LOONS*

Shoemaker and the Lovebird

It would have come as a surprise to nobody if Shoemaker's wife and daughter had an unfortunate mishap during the family vacation. Bets were cast around the water cooler at work as to the method he might employ to off his wife. Employees and management alike expected to turn on CNN or some other major news affiliate and see his dismal face plastered across the big screen as the authorities leveled charges and hauled him away.

To prevent any mishaps, days before the cruise, Shoemaker secretly visited a psychotherapist. He sought advice on how to survive his wife's insufferable nagging and daughter's continual whining during the weeklong trip.

"Sedatives," Doctor Moon advised. He scribbled his initials on a paper and handed the prescription to Shoemaker. "Most of my patients refer to them as happy pills. These things could anesthetize a horse."

Shoemaker vibrantly shook the doctor's hand. "I can't thank you enough. My wife has the personality of a stale bean."

"Please," Moon interrupted. "I'm married. Tell me something I don't know."

The cruise ship, named the Lovebird, was scheduled to set sail from Baltimore.

Upon arrival, Shoemaker's daughter insisted they eat at a sushi bar, if for no other reason, sushi made him nauseous. Much like the cuisine at Alfred's Diner, it brought on awkward bouts of gastritis.

After a grueling session in the bathroom, they hailed a cab to drive them to port. Upon exiting the taxi, Shoemaker's wife tossed an arsenal of luggage at him, and then yapped irritably in his ear when he lagged behind.

Still the vacation remained tolerable. The sedatives prescribed by Doctor Moon continued to bolster Shoemaker's endurance and neutralize an onslaught of nagging by his irksome family.

The first several days of the cruise he pretended to be asleep all the time, only sneaking out for food after his wife and daughter retired. Other times he found himself sniggering under the bed covers for no reason at all. He surmised that either the salty ocean air washed away his stress or the medication prescribed by Doctor Moon had further fogged his already anesthetized mind.

Whatever the reprieve, Shoemaker's fragile world of calm came to an abrupt end on the third night aboard the Lovebird when his wife stung him in the head with a bra strap, waking him from a sound sleep.

"What's this?" She held up the bottle of sedatives prescribed by Doctor Moon that she found while rummaging through her husband's personal belongings.

"Medicine," he said. "The ocean water gives me the runs."

"Don't lie to me, Ed Shoemaker," she warned, bra strap in hand.

"Drugs. Is that what you want me to say, I'm taking drugs?"

Shoemaker's daughter burst into tears. "My father is a junkie!"

"Here's what I think about your irritable bowel."

His wife marched over to the commode. She tossed the sedatives in the hole and flushed.

Shoemaker gasped. He raced to the toilet but his efforts were futile. Doctor Moon's happy pills, that minuscule link to an otherwise mournful existence, now rolled through a mass of dirty pipes that would be ultimately dumped in the sea.

The next few days proved more turbulent than the unsteady waves of the ocean. At dinner, his daughter complained to strangers about her father. His wife aided in the abuse by claiming she was married to an insensitive louse with a fetish for illegal narcotics. Any measure of rest became impossible. One morning Shoemaker woke to find that his daughter flung her panties across the room and they landed on his face. Bras and feminine hygiene utilities littered the cabin. He even found traces of his wife's clipped toenails in his shaving kit.

Stress, like a volcano, built.

One night, after his wife and daughter went out for the evening, Shoemaker woke up from pretending to be asleep. Grumbling to himself, he blamed most of his troubles on people like Jack Snaggler and Bob Wetterman. After the company cancelled vacations, the duo of ingrates fought to have the policy reinstated. Instead of sitting back at the office doing nothing, here he was, on the vacation of a lifetime, with a family that sported all the personality of a tree trunk.

Grabbing a pencil off the night table, he scribbled Snaggler and Wetterman's names across the wall beside his cot, then ended the graffiti with a dramatic exclamation point.

Tense as a stretched rubberband, Shoemaker decided to get some fresh air. He took a walk on the deck in hopes of staving off his irritation. Soon he found himself standing at the entrance of Shaky Jake's Rumba Lounge, an onboard dance club.

Inside the door, he caught sight of his tipsy wife mambo dancing on a tabletop. A foreigner with a shaved head and loud kabana shirt swung his hips against her to the beat of the music.

Shoemaker considered the idea that the foreigner might take a legitimate interest in his wife. Perhaps they'd even elope to Switzerland or some other remote part of the world, never to be heard from again. But logic dictated otherwise. After spending any length of time with the woman, who in their right mind would want her?

Making matters worse, Shoemaker's underage daughter stood over by the bar. She flirted with a cabin boy who found it impossible to stop touching her ass.

"Another round of margaritas!" his smashed wife yelled. She flashed a credit card around the room that had been filched from her husband's wallet.

Shoemaker rushed in and snatched the plastic card from his wife's hand. "Have you gone mad? You're draining my bank account!"

"Lighten up, imbecile." She sipped her drink then splashed the rest of it in her husband's face.

Shoemaker wiped himself with a napkin, all the while the festive crowd jeered and mocked.

"I'm leaving," he announced and stormed off like an angry bull.

"Where do you think you're going? You're on a boat in the middle of the ocean, you klutz," his wife mocked.

The foreigner with the shaved head repeatedly grabbed Shoemaker's arm as he made his exit. "I didn't know she was married, pal. She came up to me and wanted to get cozy. It's all good, right?"

"All good?" Shoemaker pulled his arm away. "Take her to a ranch and saddle her up like a mule for all I care. I'm leaving."

Shoemaker's wife stood up on a chair and pointed a finger from across the room. "Don't you dare disobey me and walk out that door."

Refusing to comply, Shoemaker turned and stuck his tongue out then hurried out the exit. His scorned wife dashed after him shouting obscenities every step of the way.

Outside the bar, Shoemaker slipped on a freshly scrubbed floor and did a tumbleset into a public hot tub. Two women in string bikinis drank champagne in the bubbly water. They screamed at Shoemaker's unexpected intrusion. Sopping wet, he quickly climbed out of the tub and kept moving.

Bystanders would later recount seeing a drenched man, giggling madly and answering to Shoemaker's description, run by them while an irate woman with a foul mouth and a lime margarita chased after him.

When Shoemaker's wife arrived back at the cabin, her husband was nowhere to be found. Crabby and drunk, she vowed to deal with him in the morning. Shoemaker's daughter spent the night with the cabin boy who kept touching her ass. She never did come home until after sunrise.

In the morning, after a shower, breakfast, a little shopping and sunbathing, Ed Shoemaker was still counted among the missing. His wife concluded it was time to alert security. The crew doggedly searched every inch of the ship but found no trace of the misplaced passenger.

Alarmed at the prospects of a lawsuit, the captain of the Lovebird notified the authorities about the mishap. Investigators met Shoemaker's wife at the next available port.

"Tell us everything." One of the detectives handed her a tissue to blow her nose. "Did your husband suffer from any emotional problems?"

"Sometimes he grew irritable." She snuffled. "It's almost as if something grated on his nerves. I found a controlled substance in his baggage. He was a non-recovering addict."

Witnesses onboard were detained and questioned. The foreigner with the shaved head attested to dancing in a bar with Shoemaker's wife on the night of the disappearance. "I didn't know his wife. She put the move on me in the bar," he told authorities. "The next thing I know she's balancing a margarita in her hand and chasing him across the main deck. I'm betting suicide."

Standing by the bow of the ship, Shoemaker's wife again burst into tears. Her whiny voice screeched like a wounded seagull.

"We're following all leads." The detective offered assurance and tried to shut her up. "If it's any consolation," he looked into the calm of the sea, "he's probably at peace now."

"Hey chief," the detective's partner hollered. He leaned over a rail around a hot tub near the portside of the ship, just outside Shaky Jake's Rumba Lounge. "I think you better take a look at this. There's something floating in the water."